TEN PERCENT OF MY HEART

A NOVEL

STACY LEE

WHAT READERS ARE SAYING!

I was so excited to dive into Stacy Lee's new book, Ten Percent of my Heart, I love her Nubble Lighthouse series! From the first page I was hooked with Tessa and her love story, but **I also love how she wove the characters from her other books into this one and we got a quick update into everyone's love lives.** This is a love story between mothers, between what our heart wants, but more importantly how our choices shape not only our lives but everyone who plays a part in it. I can't wait to read the next book in this series!

— KATIE BRESSACK—READER

Once again Stacy Lee has given us an engaging story of love, life and lessons learned! *Ten Percent of my Heart* captured me from the moment I read the first page. You are reunited with Cassidy and Sean as they help to tell the story of Tessa. **Through a series of unexpected twists, you become immersed in Tessa's life, emotions, and journey to understand the importance of listening to your heart and doing what makes you happy.** *Ten Percent of my Heart* is another incredible addition to the Nubble Light Series, set in the beautiful backdrop of York Beach, Maine making this book a must read!

— BRIANA WOMACK—READER

PRAISE FOR THE NUBBLE LIGHT SERIES BY STACY LEE

"The author has a unique style of writing. She has her story development under control, no matter the twist that she adds at any point... I'd rate it **four out of four stars.**"

— -ONLINE BOOK CLUB

Lee offers skillful plotting that unveils several surprises readers won't see coming, both in the thriller and romance departments."

— -KIRKUS REVIEW

"I could see the Nubble Lighthouse in the distance. When the characters walked through the sandy beaches falling in love or experiencing heartbreak, I, too, could hear the music wafting over from the nearby piano bar."

— -ALLISON NOWAK- REEDSY

"I was so engrossed in this book that I forgot to eat. The suspense it contained is top-notch. I must commend the author for this masterpiece."

— - ELENDU EKECHUKWU- READER

The characters and events in this book are fictitious. All of the characters, organizations, and events portrayed in this novel are either products of the author's imagination or are used fictitiously. Any similarity to real persons, living or dead, is coincidental and not intended by the author.

TEN PERCENT OF MY HEART by Stacy Lee

Copyright © 2022 by Stacy Lee

French Martini Press

Salem, New Hampshire

All rights reserved. In accordance with the U.S. Copyright Act of 1976, the scanning, uploading, and electronic sharing of any part of this book without the permission of the publisher constitute unlawful privacy and theft of the author's intellectual property. If you would like to use the material from the book (other than for review purposes), prior written permission must be obtained by contacting the publisher at frenchmartinipress@gmail.com. Thank you for the support of the author's rights.

❦ Created with Vellum

For my son, Paul. Follow your heart, Dear.

A NOTE TO THE READER

This is the fourth book in the Nubble Light series. The first book, *The Hundredth Time Around*, was published in January of 2021. *Future Plans* is the second book in the series and was released in April of 2021. *Never in a Billion* is the third book and was released in December of 2021. Book five is already in the works! Although each book in the Nubble Light series can stand alone, I highly encourage you to read them in order, beginning with *The Hundredth Time Around*, especially prior to reading *Ten Percent of My Heart*.

The Nubble Light series was inspired by my visit to York Beach in 2020. My mother-in-law, Shirley Barbagallo, brought my family and me to visit during what ended up being some of the last months of her life. During this visit, we fell in love with the beaches of York, Maine, Cape Neddick, and the Nubble Lighthouse. Because of this, the Nubble Lighthouse holds a special place in my heart.

Also, please be on the lookout for a special short series I am writing for elementary-school-aged children from the point of view of dogs at daycare. Please visit www.stacyleeauthor.com for more information.

ACKNOWLEDGMENTS

I am truly blessed to be living my dream as a full-time author, and I am overcome with gratitude for the many incredible individuals I have been blessed with along the way. A big thank you to Lynn and her team at Red Adept Editing. I couldn't do this without you! Also, another huge thank you to Julie and her team at Spark Creative for designing yet another gorgeous cover. Thank you, Kris and the team, at the Talking Book. Collaborating with you, Anne-Marie Lewis, and John York on the audiobook production of the Nubble Light series has been truly fantastic. A special thank you to Allen Redwing and the team at Bookscribs. I can't wait to see the Nubble Light series on the big screen! Thank you, Roxanne Hiatt, for your assistance with marketing and navigating social media campaigns. Thank you to the team at eBook Marketing Solutions. It is truly amazing to see *Future Plans* and *Never in a Billion* hit the Amazon best seller list! Thank you, Brian Feinblum and Media Kit Buzz, Inc., for your guidance and support in the areas of marketing and promotion. I have learned so much from you and can't wait to put it all into action!

I could never do this without the love and support of my family! To my husband, Paul Barbagallo, thank you for believing in me, encouraging me, and being my rock. I love you with one hundred percent of my heart and couldn't do this without you. Thank you to my children, Paul and Lucy. I am so proud of both of you and love watching you live your dreams! Congratulations, Paul, on your admittance to Central Catholic High School. We are going to be the loudest, most embarrassing parents in the stands at your football games. We are ready to Raider! Lucy, we are so proud of your accomplishments, on the stage and off. Keep up the great work!

A very special thank you to my family, friends, and faithful support system. My parents, Karen and Dan DeBruyckere; sister, Kate Giglio, and her husband, Joe; my sister-in-law, Cheri Grassi, and her husband, Mike; my aunt, Pat Fishwick; and my brother, Dan DeBruyckere Jr. Thank you, Kara Holloway, Stacie Swanson, Jess Delano, and Marisa Berlin, for your encouragement and friendship. Thank you, Jaclyn Hannan and Aaron Pawelek, for your constant guidance and support. I wouldn't be where I am today without you! Jaclyn, thank you for bringing me back to my *Dawson's Creek* days… just in time… and Aaron, thank you for your ideas pertaining to #mapoftheirlives. Thank you, Rob Hulse, for letting me pick your brain about dating terminology and logistics in 2022… I sure have learned a lot! Thank you for everything you have done for my family, for kicking my butt into shape, and for making me better.

Thank you to the community of York Beach, Maine, and the Cape Neddick Community. You have been so receptive to the Nubble Light series, and I can't thank you enough for your support. A special thank you to the gift shops in York and Ogunquit, Maine. Whispering Sands, Beach Funatic, the Nubble Lighthouse Giftshop, and the Ogunquit Drug Store.

Of course, I need to thank you, the reader! Thank you for reading my novels and for your feedback. It brings such joy to my heart that you are falling in love with the characters and feel like they are your friends. May you continue to love without hesitation and dream the biggest dreams… Remember, nothing is impossible. There is always a way if you follow your heart. I hope you enjoy book four of the Nubble Light series. Thank you, and God bless!

PROLOGUE

It hadn't been my intention to fall in love. Why would anyone willingly go out of their way to overcomplicate a picture-perfect life? I am already in love, fully committed to another person. Of course, relationships take work... and although mine has its challenges, we are in a solid place. We are happy... or at least I like to believe that we are.

I've learned that having feelings for a person, whether that be love, lust, or simply increased dopamine and norepinephrine levels in our brains... is still *real*. It doesn't play fair, and it surely doesn't play nice. You see, love doesn't take turns. It isn't like the methodical and systematic line for the ladies' room, women filing in one after the other, taking turns as stalls become vacant. And it isn't like moving over in your seat on the bus or the subway, allowing someone else to share space that was comfortably yours. No. When you are already in love and your heart has been fully given to another person, there just isn't enough space for you to fully fall in love with another. It isn't possible, or even fair for that matter, for a person in this predicament to have their cake and eat it too.

So, if I can't very well dedicate ninety percent of my heart to one person and ten percent to another, where does that leave me? I'll tell you where... determined to shed that extra piece of my soul that has me completely and utterly paralyzed with emotions that were *not* invited. I need to let them go, and I will move on. I don't have a choice because it's not only about me anymore. There is just too much at stake to give in to this desire. It is time to consider my future... our future.

I've been told that pain is weakness leaving the body. If that's true, I'm getting stronger by the second. This whole thing, it isn't easy... it's terrifying. We get one shot at this life we live. And this hurt... this loss... these emotions... these tears... they are one hundred percent real. I'll probably be crying those tears forever. Because for the first time in my life, I am backing down from something I want. For the first time in the history of my existence, I am burying a dream.

This ten percent of me... this tiny part that is clinging on for dear life to the distorted possibility of things working out between us could destroy me. So, I'll smile... I'll live... I'll love. And I will fill that tiny void with the joy that comes from watching my child grow, hearing that laugh, experiencing motherhood. No matter how strong a connection I share with that man and what sort of joy he could have brought to my life, it ends *now*.

Timing can be everything... and in this case, it is my enemy. As these tears trickle down my cheeks like they do day after day, month after month, and probably year after year, I will rest in the knowledge that even though they sting, even though I'll always be a little empty on the inside... I will be whole in other ways... ways I once only imagined. So, to the love that will never be, the love that can never be one hundred percent mine, I will see you in my dreams. Because selfishly, those will always belong to me.

IN THE FUTURE -

WRITER SALT PODCAST WITH SEAN ANDERSON

Sean: Welcome to *Writer Salt*, a podcast for authors who, like me, sometimes just need to hear a good old-fashioned love story from time to time to get those creative juices flowing.

Cassidy: (laughing)

Sean: Um... did I say something funny, Cass?

Cassidy: *Creative juices.* It just struck me as an odd choice in words. Besides, your show isn't just for authors. It's also for those of us who like a good old-fashioned *love story*. I should know— I've listened to every episode.

Sean: (chuckles)

Cassidy: Sorry. It took long enough for you to invite me on the show; I should probably behave.

Sean: No need to apologize.

Cassidy: Thanks, Sean.

Sean: As you can see, my wife, Cassidy, will be joining us today. Totally not an author, most definitely an attorney... a stickler for details... which I suppose can be both a blessing and a curse. Anyhow, I brought her on today to help me with some promo, but it looks as though she's taking over.

Cassidy: (flirtatiously) Well, I *am* the inspiration behind your books, so it's only right.

Sean: I can't argue with that... but they've heard our story already... you know, one hundred dollars for one hundred days, old dusty trunk in the attic... an unusual and twisted sort of family tree... so go for it, Cass... why don't you talk about the *book*... then we can introduce our guest.

Cassidy: Gotcha. As Sean mentioned, I'm joining you today to tell you about the release of Sean Anderson's book, titled *Ten Percent of my Heart*. It's the fourth book in his series, Stories of the Nubble Light, and you really won't want to miss this one. I'm super proud of him! (Kissing noise).

Sean: (chuckles) Thanks, Cass. And although my beautiful wife has inspired this series, someone else that is very special to us was the muse for the fourth book, and we are super pumped to have her on the show today.

Cassidy: (excited squeal) She is *truly* amazing.

Sean: Our friend Tessa has agreed to join us today. Her story is probably one of the most powerful and heroic tales of love and sacrifice thus far, and we can't wait for you to hear from her.

Tessa: Thank you, guys! I've never done anything like this before, and I appreciate you having me on your show. I love the Nubble Light books, and I am so grateful to call you both my friends.

Sean: The feeling is mutual, for sure. Thank you for coming on and for sharing your story. I think everyone is going to love it... almost as much as we do. So... let's get to it... Why don't you start from the beginning?

Tessa: The very beginning?

Sean: The *very* beginning.

Tessa: Well... I guess it all started in 2016, back when I *thought* I had it all. My whole life was ahead of me. (sighs)... I was in love. There was legit a proposal right around the corner. I mean, there was even a ring... and then... I guess it all just came crashing down around me. *Total* change of course, if you know what I mean?

Sean: Yes, we do know what you mean. Sounds familiar... right, Cass?

Cassidy: I can *totally* relate to that.

Tessa: Right? I read Sean's first book before I even got to know you. It blew me away, even then. I could totally relate to what you went through.

Sean: We all get knocked down hard sometimes, that's for sure... and you sure did get knocked down good. So, what did you do in that moment? When you had nothing left to give? What was it that changed it around?

Tessa: He did. *He* changed it around. He changed *everything*... and you know what? I wouldn't have it any other way.

IN THE PAST

TESSA

March 2016

"I'm sorry, I don't mean to pry, but I need to know… Who does your hair?"

I flinched, startled at this question, since I was hyperfocused on the bathroom mirror, battling a pesky ground pepper grain that had weaseled its way in between my two front teeth. "Heh?" I muttered as I continued performing minor surgery with my thumbnail. *This could be the most important night of my life, and I refuse to spend one more second of it in this bathroom, picking at my teeth.*

"Your hair," the woman reiterated, only when she asked the question this time, she plucked a toothpick from her Dooney and Bourke crossbody bag and released it into my open hand. Suddenly, although we had never actually met before, I silently declared this stranger my new best friend.

"Oh… oh my goodness," I gasped, accepting her precious gift, and declaring victory over the pepper grain. I presented my shiny pearly whites to the mirror and breathed a relieved sigh. "Thank you so much, really. This... is an important night..."

She inched closer, slowly, until the mirror presented both our reflections. She was stunning in just about every way. She towered over me by at least three inches, her legs seeming to go on for miles. She gathered her brunette hair over one shoulder and compared it to mine, acting like she had known me forever.

"Our natural colors are similar, and I have been looking to, I don't know... lighten everything up a bit."

I realized that she was referring to the thick caramel-brown highlights I had invested a ton of money (that I didn't have) in just days prior, convinced that *this* was it. This was the night that Noah would propose. I had discovered the engagement ring accidentally. I was rummaging through the glove compartment of his firecracker-red Jeep Wrangler, hoping to find spare change for a fundraiser at work, when I found the tiny black velvet box tucked away between his automobile registration and a bottle of Axe body spray. I sprang back, shocked to say the least. After five whole minutes of telling myself to breathe, I snapped it open. My almond-shaped copper-colored eyes bugged out of my head while my jaw had all but dropped to the floor. "A twisted halo platinum emerald cut engagement ring... *no way.*" The diamond was well over a carat, way larger than we had discussed when daydreaming of our future together. We had often discussed the intricate details of things like wedding bands, honeymoon destinations, and of course, which expensive espresso machine we would select for our Target gift registry.

"Was it locally?"

"Locally?"

"Your hairstylist?"

"Yes," I replied, stumbling awkwardly out of my daydream. "I go to Liz over at that little salon in downtown Plymouth," I explained, silently cursing myself that thoughts of my engagement ring were encompassing my entire being so I couldn't think of the name of the place where I had gotten my hair cut since my freshman year of college. "You know... the one near that cute little coffee shop just over the bridge."

"I know just the one you are talking about. Do you live here, in Plymouth?"

Our eyes remained locked on the mirror as she matched my highlighted tresses against her fair complexion. "I do," I said, holding still like a statue, very aware that this moment was a bit awkward but also caught off guard by how familiar it felt. "I went to Plymouth State University, and now I rent an apartment on my own, right off campus."

My new friend released my hair from her fingers and brushed it gently back in place. "How lovely," she declared. "Did you meet at school?"

I rummaged through my bag and retrieved my favorite lip gloss. I applied it generously, suddenly eager to get back to Noah and the cozy corner booth in the back of our favorite Italian restaurant. "Yes. He graduated a few years ahead of me... I guess I just really like New Hampshire." I shrugged, offering more information than was asked of me, a nervous habit of mine. "It was really nice to meet you... I'm sorry... I didn't get your name?"

"Sam," she stated blissfully. "It was nice to meet you. If I were you, I wouldn't keep your date waiting."

"Right," I said, backing up toward the door, her eyes still locked on mine. "Thank you... you know... for the toothpick. You truly are a lifesaver."

I adjusted the bottom of my black cocktail dress and exited the bathroom. I scurried past the bar area and down the familiar restaurant hallway and noticed that it was unusually busy for a Thursday night. I smiled, eager to get back to Noah, who sat perched against the wall in our favorite corner booth of the farmhouse-style restaurant. As I approached our table, he smiled at me and puckered his lips together, gesturing for a kiss. I placed my purse on the seat across from him and gathered my hair over one shoulder to keep it from landing in the remaining marinara from his well-enjoyed chicken parmesan dinner.

"Hey, babe," I whispered softly just before my lips pressed against his and automatically curled into a soft smile. I paused there for a beat, inhaling the familiar scent of his aftershave mixed with the aroma of Italian cuisine. "You smell yummy."

He kissed my nose, one of his classic moves. "I was starting to worry about you," he said as he pulled back from our kiss.

"Little old me?" I sang and plopped down into my seat across from him. He smiled in the boyish way he often did and studied me intently.

"Yes, little old you," he said, his tone softening a bit. "You look beautiful, as always." He secured his hands around mine, giving them a gentle squeeze. I studied him like a detective trying to crack a major case. *Will he propose? Tonight?* He guided my hand slowly toward his lips and kissed my fingers before releasing them. I rubbed his arm with my open palm, not failing to notice the way his black cotton polo shirt clung to his biceps in all the right ways.

"You're looking pretty nice too." I reached over and ran my hand playfully over his short and needly tresses. I admired his military-style clean buzz cut and fresh shave. He beamed at me with his irresistible green eyes, and I wondered how on Earth I could possibly be this lucky. Out of all the colleges in the entire world, Noah and I ended up choosing the same one. My heart fluttered expectedly, and my knee involuntarily bounced under the table in anticipation of what was to come.

"So, Tess... there is, uh... something I've been meaning to talk to you about."

My shoulders tightened toward my ears, and I sat up straighter than I had intended. *Stay calm, Tessa,* I silently scolded. I searched his familiar eyes for reassurance that this was really happening and found nothing but evidence that yes, this was most definitely happening. Any moment now, Noah Clark could transition from being my boyfriend—my college sweetheart—to my actual *fiancé*... a moment I had been waiting for since the day we met. "Something good, I hope?"

"Oh yeah." He chuckled. "It's good." Tiny beads of sweat formed on the creases of his forehead, and his eyes locked on mine. Noah cleared his throat and dabbed his forehead with his dinner napkin. I gazed in awe as he reached into the pocket of his tan khaki dress pants, his smile growing larger and joy shooting from his eyeballs like lightning bolts... and then— he froze... like a *freaking statue.* The childish excitement that had just moments ago encompassed his entire being just... vanished. I followed his gaze and whipped my head to the side, expecting to see someone behind me, but it was just us.

"Noah? What's wrong?"

"It's nothing," he said, clearing his throat once again as his empty hands returned to the tabletop. He pumped his fist against his chest and swallowed. "Just a little heartburn. That red sauce gets me every time, right?"

But I had not wished to discuss his indigestion just then. I cleared my own throat and shook my head as waves of uneasiness began to take over my entire being. "Here," I said, offering him my water. He sipped it eagerly as I reached for my wineglass, already sipping my chardonnay before speaking. "Maybe next time you should try the alfredo?"

He smiled and dabbed his mouth with his napkin. "You're always thinking. That's what I love about you, Tessa."

"Right... You were saying?"

"Saying?"

"You had something to ask me?" I held my breath and pressed down on my knee to stop its involuntary bouncing. I glanced down at my newly manicured fingernails, already envisioning that engagement ring sliding over my knuckle, and suddenly becoming more impatient than I expected.

"Right, I did. Sorry about that. It's about next weekend."

"Next weekend?"

"Justin from the office is renting out his house in North Conway. He has availability for next weekend. I was hoping that maybe you felt like getting away together?"

"Of course," I said, allowing the last drop of wine to trickle down the glass. "That sounds perfect," I said, presenting Noah with the most enthusiastic smile I could manage in the moment.

IN THE PAST

TESSA

April 2016

"He *didn't* propose?"

"Not so loud!" I scolded Ramona. "The kids are coming in from morning recess. Just... I don't know, close the door or something." I shoved my face between my diamond-less fingers and mustered up a dramatic grunt.

Ramona kicked my office door closed with the bottom of her white Converse sneaker and curled her lips into a sarcastic smile. "What if the kids need their guidance counselor?"

"What if the guidance counselor needs a guidance counselor?" I muffled into my hands. I rubbed my tired eyes, remorseful that I allowed the proposal's intensity (or lack thereof) to take away so much needed sleep. How could I have been *so* convinced that he was going to pop the question at dinner? How long could I possibly go on like this? "Don't you have to get to class?"

She glanced at the clock on my desk. "I have a whole six minutes left."

"Ramona, you are my older and *wiser* work friend. You would tell me if I were overreacting, wouldn't you?" I tugged at my disheveled, messy bun and stared at her, my eyes wide.

Ramona leaned against my desk and sipped her coffee. "Because I love you, Tessa, I am going to pretend that you didn't just call me old."

"You know what I mean. I just turned twenty-three, and you have… you know… life experience. Being in your forties doesn't make you old… just wise."

"Okay, let's think this through. You thought he was planning on proposing, and when he reached into his pocket, the ring wasn't there?"

I rolled my eyes. "Noah doesn't even show up to frat parties empty handed. You think he would orchestrate a proposal without a ring?"

"Or," she continued, obviously ignoring me, "maybe he really did have heartburn?"

"He does get bad indigestion when he eats acidic foods."

"Listen, I know how much you care about Noah and how convinced you are that he is going to propose, but I don't know, Tessa. I feel like, yeah… you might be forcing this one just a bit."

"I know. I would tell anyone else the same thing." I sucked my iced coffee through the straw at record speed to get the caffeine pumping through my veins before the morning began. "It's just that he's the one. I know it. But… I guess you're right."

Ramona placed a reassuring hand on my shoulder. "You have your whole life ahead of you, sweetie. Enjoy what you have going for you! There will be plenty of time for marriage and a family… all the things I know you want. Think of it this way. When you go home and leave these kids behind, you don't have three waiting for you at home like I do. I would literally die for your freedom. Hey... don't you have some fun plans coming up this weekend?"

I nodded but was focused on sucking up the remaining sugar at the bottom of my plastic cup. I crunched the sugar between my teeth and smiled with satisfaction. "I'm heading into Boston with some friends from school," I explained, suddenly eager to get this Friday over with. "You're right," I admitted. "I'm rushing things. I need to dial it back."

I rested my chin in my hands and studied the photographs on my desk, particularly the one of Noah and me from our summer vacation. The picture was taken by the Nubble Lighthouse, a place that was near and dear to my family, my childhood home. In the picture, Noah held me on his back in a piggyback. My arms were wrapped around his neck, my cheek pressed against his. His blond hair glistened in the sun against the Nubble's glow.

"Well... what advice *would* you give someone else?"

Ramona loved to play this game. It was almost as if she was testing the knowledge I gained and the necessary skills I acquired as a social worker against me... and she enjoyed it. I rolled my eyes and smacked my hand against my forehead. "Ramona! I haven't had enough coffee for this."

She ran her fingers through her short black bob and chewed her bottom lip, clearly not letting me off the hook. "What advice would you give?" Her voice was steady, and I had no choice but to give in. I relaxed my shoulders and breathed in heavily. "I... I would..."

My sentence was interrupted by the school bell's ear-piercing ring. Ramona leaped back, almost tripping over my conference table. "Third grade calls!" she sang as she exited my office. "Keep your chin up. That boy loves you—I can tell. This love story has a happy ending, I just know it."

I nodded in agreement and prayed she was right—

because a piece of me was convinced, with all my heart, that Noah was head over heels in love with me, while the other part, that part that seemed to be surfacing more and more lately, was screaming at me, like the school bell, that not all love stories had happy endings.

* * *

THE CLOCK'S tick-tock reminded me, with every quick bite of my salad, that my twenty-two-minute lunch break would be over in just a moment. My left hand worked quickly to respond to my sister-in-law over text, while the other worked away at my salad—multitasking at its finest.

Kayla: I'm confused. Did he not have the ring in his pocket?

Tessa: WHO.EVEN.KNOWS?!

Kayla: You are *sure* that he was proposing?

Tessa: YES. The guy was sweating bullets. He never sweats.

Kayla: Was his food too spicy or something?

Tessa: Nooooooo! I'm telling you...he was proposing... and then he just WASN'T.

Kayla: That's odd. Did you have food in your teeth or something?

I GRIMACED and slammed my phone down, harder than I intended. If I hadn't been so confused about Noah and his proposal fake-out, I would have laughed at the irony of Kayla's message. A soft knock on the door of my office interrupted my thoughts. "Hi, Miss Walker," a meek little voice called from the doorway.

"Bex!" I cheered in the overly enthusiastic way I often did when I greeted my favorite first-grader. "Come in, buddy!"

Bex pushed through the seemingly heavy door and closed it behind him. He took a seat at my short, round conference table and placed his binder and lunchbox in front of him as he had done every day since September. "How was recess?"

He shrugged and smirked a little, wiping dark-brown bangs to the side. His little but careful brown eyes grew wide, like he had something to tell me but couldn't quite find the words. Beckett (Bex for short) had been diagnosed with social anxiety and sensory modulation and integration disorder when he was in kindergarten. He had struggled in class, especially when it came to making friends and working in groups. His parents had suggested retaining him for one more year to help with his confidence, but his academic test scores were simply way too high. Instead of keeping him back, we decided to increase his interventions, the most significant being time with me, the school guidance counselor, and luckily I was able to help him. "I bet it's getting warm outside?"

"Yes," he agreed.

"What did you have for lunch today?" I asked, gesturing toward his New England Patriots lunch box.

"Cheese sandwich," he whispered, like he was giving away a juicy secret.

"Did you eat it all?"

He unzipped his lunchbox as he did each afternoon in my office and displayed the same crusty sandwich remains as usual.

"Great job, buddy."

"Thanks, Miss Walker." His lips curved into a soft side smirk as he proudly presented a fluorescent-pink sticky note. "It's a good one."

"Mom's note?"

"Yup."

"What does it say today?"

He traced his tiny fingers over the paper. "Mommy loves you, Little Man." He grinned a toothless grin, and my heart all but melted. But then, like clockwork, his smile morphed into a pout, and his tiny eyes welled with tears. "I," he started. "I miss Mommy. I want to go home now."

I rose from my chair and made my way casually towards my conference table, already reaching for a Hershey's Kiss... Bex's favorite. "What time does my clock say?"

"Twelve thirty."

"How long until you will see Mommy?"

"Two hours."

"That's right," I stated firmly, as I had done every day at this time. "And time flies when..."

"When you're having fun!"

"Tell me more about recess, Bex. I bet it was really muddy!"

He nodded and giggled for a beat, his eyes locked on the candy. "Yes. But mud is gross."

I tossed the Hershey's Kiss towards him, and he caught it with both hands. "Was the kickball field closed? Because of the mud?"

He opened the wrapper and began chomping on the candy as if it was the greatest thing he had ever tasted. "Yes."

I pulled up a chair next to Bex and reached for his binder. His short sweatpants-covered legs dangled above the tile floor as he chewed the candy, tiny bits of chocolate drool appearing on the corners of his mouth. I handed him a napkin and instructed him to wipe his face. "All right, Bex, you know the drill. You need to tell me who you played with at recess, and we write it here, in the binder."

"I went on the swings."

"Great," I sang, already jotting in the notes. "With whom?"

"SpongeBob SquarePants," he declared confidently and then burst out laughing... belly laughing, and for a moment I hoped he had successfully swallowed his candy. "April Fool's!"

"Chew your candy, Little Monkey," I warned. "But yes, you got me! Good one! Today is the first day of April. Man, you got me good!"

He nodded, clearly very proud of himself.

"Now let's get to work. Who did you play with outside today? And *don't* say an overly enthusiastic sponge who lives in a pineapple under the sea."

IN THE PAST

TESSA

April 2016

It had been a week since the proposal that never was. Noah had been going about his business as usual. He was still staying at my apartment most nights, even though it meant an extra thirty-minute commute to his high school, where he taught biology. Teaching high school science was his dream job, and he scored a position at the school because of another teacher's maternity leave right out of his student teaching. The position remained vacant the following year, which allowed him to stay. We both felt fortunate, walking into the jobs of our dreams. It had felt like the first steps in the right direction toward our future together.

But there was no way of telling what was going through that mind of his. If he could sense trouble in paradise, he never let on. I did, however, make it a point to stop at CVS multiple times that week for his antacids. My concern for his esophagus may have seemed a bit over the top... or maybe just a bit passive-aggressive... Either way, the guy had to know something was up.

Noah and I had met in college my freshman year and his junior. Although we had shared the same biology and psychology classes and even sat at the same table sometimes, it wasn't until a night out at the local pub that we exchanged any sort of dialogue.

"Has anyone ever told you that you look *just* like Rachel Bilson?"

I was tongue-tied to say the least. Rachel Bilson was one of my absolute favorite actresses, and to hear the guy I had been crushing on for over a month tell me I *looked* like her was beyond crazy. "Me? Rachel Bilson? Either you've had too much to drink, or you've lost your mind..." His eyes locked on mine, and for a second, I felt like the wind had been sucked out of me.

"You look just like her."

"Yeah, okay. That's what you tell all the girls."

He swiveled toward me on his barstool, one elbow on the table and the other on his hip. "Sweetheart," he stated with confidence. "Let me assure you... there are no other girls."

Ironically, that was the only time in our entire relationship that Noah referred to me as "sweetheart." But that night, the night I officially met Noah Clark... it changed my entire life. I had informed him that he was the spitting image of Channing Tatum—because he was. And before I knew it, we were hand in hand, heading up the stairs to his apartment, which was conveniently above the happening pub scene. And that night, two college kids in Plymouth New Hampshire fell in love.

That had been years ago, and as I pulled back the covers of the queen-sized bed in my one-bedroom apartment, post non-proposal, I felt comfort in remembering that night. I kept telling myself that it wasn't like Noah had done anything wrong. If I hadn't discovered the ring in the glove compartment of his jeep, last week's dinner would have simply just been another night out... Noah and Tessa out for a quiet dinner at their favorite spot. But I couldn't shake the questions that zoomed through my brain at a million miles per hour. I knew Noah better than I knew anybody else... and I would have bet my life that he was about to propose. I couldn't help but wonder, what changed his mind? Was it something I had said? Was it the obnoxious way that my knee involuntarily shook under the table? Was it his *mother*? I knew that I wasn't her favorite person in the entire world, and he was constantly striving to please her, but was that really a deal breaker for the love of your life? I wanted desperately to trust Noah, but given the current circumstances surrounding the ring and what seemed like a change of heart, that was becoming increasingly difficult by the second... and then I had the thought... which I was sure was plastered over my entire face. *What if the ring wasn't meant for me?*

"Everything okay, Tess?"

"Me? Uh, yeah. I'm okay."

"Heading to bed early, aren't you?"

"I have a meeting in the morning before school starts."

"You sure you want me to stay over?" He didn't typically ask that, and just then, I became aware that he, too, was feeling some sort of tension between us.

"Yeah. I'm sure."

Noah climbed into bed next to me, just as I pulled the covers up over my shoulders. I remained curled up on my side, snuggling against my pillow, as he shimmied closer to me. He got so close that as he spoke, his lips tickled the tip of my ear. "I'm sorry," he whispered.

I rolled over and faced him, searching his eyes for

answers. Maybe if I stared into them long enough, I could find a reason for his suspicious behavior. Part of me considered asking him what, exactly, he was sorry for. Another piece of me, a piece that had grown to love Noah for the man that he was, not the man I wanted him to be, decided it would be okay to let him off the hook this one time. "It's okay."

I closed my eyes and allowed myself to succumb to the way my body melted under the gentle touch of his lips against my earlobe, my cheek, my chin, and then my neck. I considered once again asking him what, exactly, he was sorry for. But then he traced my chin with the tips of his fingers and softly kissed my nose, and I melted. I allowed my head to rest back against my pillow as Noah climbed on top of me and continued kissing the crease of my neck, causing me to squirm beneath him. I opened my eyes and took all of him in as I traced my hands along his abdomen, his hips, and then back up again. With each centimeter of his skin I touched, the heaviness of my breath increased, as did my heart rate. I wrapped my arms around his lower back and tugged him closer to me, deciding that the closer I could be to this person, the better I would be. He secured his hands on either side of my face and pulled me in for a long and passionate kiss, and when he did, my fears and anxieties instantly melted away.

"I love you, Tessa," he whispered between kisses.

Noah lifted me by the waist and rolled onto his back, pulling me effortlessly on top of him. His eyes locked with mine, and for a moment I swore I could see into his soul. He lifted my T-shirt off my body in one gentle movement and tossed it to the side, allowing me to collapse my bare chest down on top of his, the warmth from his body providing an overwhelming sense of comfort.

"I love you, too, Noah. I love you too." And with that, I

surrendered, allowing myself to give in to the familiarity of his touch... of his love. And for that moment, even with all the chaos and noise in the world, Noah and I found each other in the stillness of that night... and just like that, we were *us* again.

I UNLOCKED my office door with one hand while balancing my iced coffee under my chin with the other. It pushed open easily, and I made my way briskly to my desk, where I dropped my bags with a thud. I glanced up at the clock on the wall, which read 7:45 a.m. Just enough time to organize my thoughts before my meeting.

As the school guidance counselor, I attended many meetings. Some for IEP evaluations, some for 504 plans, and others just for support. But today was a little bit different. Out of all the children I served at school in the first year of my career, Beckett Allen had been one of my favorites. I knew I wasn't supposed to have favorites, but he was just so freaking cute. And although my work with Bex had received praise from my school principal and many emails from his mother, I had never actually met Mrs. Allen. Ramona thought I was kidding when I mentioned this the day before. "You weren't at his 504 meeting? According to Phoebe Jamison, the speech pathologist, that mother was out for blood! She is a mama bear for sure," she had shrilled, forming claw hands and making a strange animal sound.

"Well, I suppose having the stomach bug has its perks," I had replied. I remembered that day crystal clear. I had awoken with a nasty stomach bug, so bad that Noah took the day off from work to be with me. I had missed an important 504 meeting, but my colleagues had taken notes, and I was able to look over the necessary paperwork from home. Plus, it hadn't been rocket science... Beckett was way too advanced to remain another year in kindergarten. He would move up to first grade with the necessary classroom accommodations, and of course, my support. That also led to multiple daily emails from Samantha Allen. I emailed Beckett's mother more than I emailed my own mother. Our email communication had originally consisted of daily conversation regarding Bex and his social goals. However, over the past few weeks, our dialogue had become more and more personal. *Thank you for everything you have done for Bex,* she wrote. *Not only has he been coming home from school with a smile on his face, but he is also actually telling me about his day! I can't ask for more... Thank you, Miss Walker.*

I didn't normally get nervous prior to parent meetings, but in this case, Mrs. Allen had specifically asked to meet with just *me.* She apparently wanted to thank me personally for my work with her son, and "pick my brain" regarding classroom placement for next year. I had been hesitant at first to meet with her alone, since her reputation preceded her, but when push came to shove, I decided that I could hold my own enough to hang with Mrs. Allen for thirty minutes, give or take a few.

"Hello?"

"Come in," I called, my back still towards the door. "Come in and have a seat..." I shoved my backpack under my desk, grabbed my coffee and my notebook, and scurried over to the conference table. "You can have a seat right here—" But my words were cut short. Because there, standing in my doorway, was the toothpick-bearing, hair-color-envying, overly friendly stranger from the bathroom last Thursday night. And she stole *my* highlights. "Sam?" I asked, the surprise in my voice not subtle at all. Simultaneously, I realized that Sam was in fact short for Samantha. Samantha Allen. "You're... you're Beckett's mother?"

"Why, yes I am. Have we met before?"

"Um... *why*, yes, we have, actually. Bathroom at the Farmhouse? Toothpick? *Highlights*," I said, grabbing a clump of my own hair and reaching it out to her, silently scolding myself for my inability to be professional in this obviously uncomfortable situation.

"That's right," she replied innocently. "I thought I recognized you from somewhere," she added, pulling out the metal chair and taking a seat at my conference table. "What are the odds?"

I studied her for a beat, wondering just exactly what the odds were that the random woman in a restaurant's bathroom during your most embarrassing night as an *un*engaged single woman really were. Especially after communicating with her via email after all these months. The woman from the bathroom, Sam/Samantha, was Beckett's mother. I cleared my throat and transitioned to the most professional voice and composure that I could muster up, still unable to forget that awkward way she held my hair in her fingers like she was my long-lost sister. "Well, let's get started, then. Will Mr. Allen be joining us?"

Her shoulders stiffened, and she sat up straighter, but her tough-as-nails expression did not waver. "He has meetings this morning. No, he won't be joining."

"That's not a problem," I reassured her. "This is a very informal meeting." I laughed nervously. I placed my open palm on my shaky knee and reached across the table, grabbing Beckett's binder. I began flipping through the pages, one after another, explaining in full detail which accommodations I had been responsible for throughout the course of her son's school day. I rambled at points, belly laughing as I explained the inside jokes we shared and games we played. I made it a point to relay the significance of her lunchbox notes and just how happy they made him. I also explained, in the most sensitive way possible, that he did really miss her throughout the school day. Her expression softened for a beat, and for a moment, I gained a glimpse into her tender side. "Do you have any questions for me, Mrs. Allen?"

"Questions?"

"Yes, questions. You know..." I realized that Mrs. Allen was not in fact listening to my presentation but instead focusing over my shoulder at the photographs on my desk.

"What a lovely picture," she said, crossing one leg over the other and sitting up even straighter. "Is that the Nubble Lighthouse? In York, Maine?"

I followed her stare until my own eyes landed on the picture—my favorite photograph of Noah and me. "Yes. I grew up in York, Maine. The Nubble, it's special to my family. My brother still lives there—"

"It's beautiful," she interrupted. "My parents were from York as well. We lived there off and on when I was a child, as did my husband's family."

"Wow! Really? Did you graduate from York High School?"

She shook her head. "No, both my husband and I went to private school."

"I see," I said, trying to remember the name of the private school that was just outside our town.

"And that's your... boyfriend?" she asked, openly checking my finger for a ring.

I felt the blood rush to my cheeks but tried my hardest to remain professional. "Yes, Noah is my boyfriend. Although," I started and stopped and started again, "I have reason to believe that he will be proposing soon." I hadn't meant to share this with her, but it felt like I needed her to know that Noah and I were not just boyfriend and girlfriend but so much more.

"Really? That's fabulous," she said, clapping her hands together. "So, he's the one?"

"Of course, yes. He's the one." I glanced over at the clock, realizing that we were running out of time. "I love that we have York in common," I said, hoping to change the subject. I began flipping through the pages of Beckett's binder once again. "Did you have any questions about placement for next year? I hate to cut this short, but the students will be coming in soon."

"No, Tessa. I don't have any questions. You have been amazing for Bex, and his father and I can't thank you enough… for everything that you have done and all you will continue to do, I'm sure of it. Oh, I suppose I should also mention that Mr. Allen and I will be out of town. We leave in two days, and we will be gone for over a week."

"Oh? Going anywhere exciting?" I asked, suddenly wondering who would take care of Bex.

"It's our anniversary," she sighed, as if explaining she had a big meeting, or heading into the doctor's office for her routine mammogram. "We are heading to Europe."

"Europe? That is so exciting!"

"Yes, well… I'm sure it will be wonderful. We don't have family in the area… Well, at least I don't. I don't trust David's side as far as I can throw them. We have a nanny… She will be just fine with Bex while we are gone. I will forward you her email address."

"I—" I started, but the sound of the morning bell interrupted me.

"That's my cue," she stated boldly. "I would hate to keep you from your work." She stood from the conference table and took one last glance at the photograph behind my desk.

"Well, you know where to find me if you do have any questions. Besides, you have my email," I say with a smile.

"Yes, I sure do. Thank you for being so efficient with the written communication. It has helped an awful lot."

"Of course," I said. "And Mrs. Allen?"

She turned toward me, one foot out the door, and adjusted her crossbody purse over her shoulder. "It's Sam. Please, call me Sam."

"Sam," I comply. "I like your highlights. They came out really great."

IN THE PAST

NOAH

April 2016

Who the hell hides an engagement ring in the glove compartment? I thought for what seemed like the hundredth time that day as I gripped the steering wheel so tightly that my knuckles turned a ghostly white color. Driving the speed limit had never really been my thing. Of course, the rule follower in me understood the importance of obeying the law and the obvious reasons for traffic safety, but something about kicking that odometer over the recommended speed limit just made me feel… I didn't know… alive?

So, on that afternoon as I drove down Route 93 with the top of my jeep down and the wind whipping around me at full speed, I felt liberated. The past couple of days had been a struggle to say the least. A part of me knew that without a doubt, Tessa had found her engagement ring. I should have known better than to keep it in the jeep. That girl didn't miss a beat. If her career as a guidance counselor didn't pan out, she could have made one hell of a detective.

Another part of me had fully intended to propose that night at dinner, and I knew that she was expecting it. I was sure that now she was questioning everything. She was smart, and her intuition was on point. I could only imagine what it had seemed like from her perspective. I was basically mid-proposal when I decided to divert from my original plan... not one of my finest moments, that's for sure. The ache in my gut grew even more painful as I planned how I could explain myself and come out the other end alive.

I flicked my blinker in preparation for exiting the highway and rehearsed the conversation over and over in my mind, not knowing just where to start but understanding that dialogue needed to happen. There were just *so* many things to consider before making a huge commitment like getting *married*. Hell, I hadn't even told her about med school yet... and I had already been *accepted*. I knew that the news would throw her for a loop. It would mean my picking up and moving from our tiny town of Plymouth, New Hampshire, to Boston... and I realized that wasn't what she was expecting... I knew this because it wasn't what we had planned. We had planned to stay in the area. We were very open about discussing the life we were planning together, and the more and more I considered my decision, the sicker I started to feel. I loved Tessa more than life itself, but if I caught her off guard like that, it was sure to be a disaster. Although she claimed to love surprises, surprises didn't really love her.

And then, of course, as much as I hated to admit it, there was the issue of my mother. I was her only child, so she had always been overly involved in my life choices. And although she claimed to be "quite sweet," I hadn't received the feedback I had hoped for after bringing Tessa to my childhood home in Concord that first Thanksgiving. I had managed to avoid inviting her home again, quite possibly because I knew there was no way it could go well, my mother being impossible to please and all. My mother was also the one who encouraged me to apply for medical school, even though I had settled into my position as a high school biology teacher. At first, I had shrugged her suggestion off like any of her other domineering slights... but then, a few weeks prior, when I read over my school contract for the following year and proceeded to sign my name... an overwhelming feeling of fear washed over me, and I just couldn't sign it.

I wasn't typically one to struggle with commitment issues. Tessa had praised me over the years for my ability to commit to my goals and persevere through even the toughest of situations. But there were just so many layers to this, so many things we hadn't had the chance to discuss, and before I misled her in any way, we would need to have a conversation. Of course, she knew that becoming a doctor had always been a dream of mine. I just didn't think that she realized that it might come before... well... us.

I pulled up to the old-fashioned white tenement where Tessa rented her one-bedroom first-floor apartment. She loved this space, but I knew more than anyone that she was eager to ditch it and move into something a little more permanent... together. I knew this because she talked about it all the time. Honesty was one of my favorite qualities about Tessa. She didn't hold back when it came to talking to me about the big and little things. The ease with which she could talk to me about anything constantly blew my mind. For me, it took time to formulate sentences to make my point in the most direct way I knew, but for Tessa it just came naturally—except for lately.

I trekked up the grassy hill to the front door of Tessa's place like I had done many times before. I reached into the pocket of my khaki pants, searching for the key to her place. I smiled softly as I remembered the night she had given it to me. We had already been dating for years, but it was the first winter in her apartment after college. We had been curled up on the carpet of her place, binge watching the TV series *24*, a small pot of Kraft Macaroni & Cheese resting between us. She scooped up the cheesy pasta with her fork, as I did with mine. "If I ever get kidnapped, you need to promise me you will send Jack Bauer to rescue me," she demanded with a mouth full of macaroni, her stare steady on the TV.

"Of course," I had said with a chuckle. "And if someone ever kidnapped you, I would find you faster than he ever could."

She had paused, scooted closer to me on the floor, and kissed me. I had closed my eyes and pulled her close for a longer kiss, and when I opened my eyes, she was dangling the key in front of me attached to a shiny silver T-shaped keychain. "For you," she had whispered. "You know, because I can't actually give *Jack Bauer* a key to my place. You will have to do, I suppose."

So, as I stuck the key into the brass doorknob of Tessa's building, the pit in my stomach grew heavier the more I rehearsed the conversation in my mind. I entered her building and sauntered down the hallway as I had many times before. I knocked on her door and started to enter as I normally would, but this time was different. This time Tessa flung the door open, her mouth gaping in horror. It only took seconds to process that she had been crying. Her dark hair was matted to her tear-streaked face, and her eyes were red and puffy. "I've been trying to call you *all* day!" she wailed.

"Tess? What's wrong?" I asked, my words coming out rushed and blended. I checked my cell phone as I walked toward her, realizing that, like an ass, I had left my cell on airplane mode all day. I had turned it on while correcting a stack of essays on endangered species and animal extinction and forgotten to switch it back. "I'm sorry," I said, rushing toward her, suddenly very worried. I couldn't help but wonder if her completely uncharacteristic behavior was connected to me and the engagement ring she had stumbled upon... or if something else could be terribly wrong. Although I didn't wish tragedy on anyone, I silently hoped that this wasn't her reaction to the obvious strain I had placed on our relationship.

"They... they died!" she blubbered, flinging her arms around my shoulders and continuing to sob into the crease of my neck.

I shook my head in confusion, struggling to comprehend who she could possibly be referring to. I wrapped one arm behind her back and the other behind her head. Her heart pounded against my chest as her sobs continued to shake her body. "Who? Who died, Tess?"

She pulled away and threw her hands to her cheeks. "A student of mine," she sobbed. "His parents... they died..."

"What? They *died?* How?"

"It was a plane crash," she choked. "It's *so* sad, Noah."

I guided her into her apartment and closed the door behind us, still struggling to process her sad news and remembering a conversation I overheard that morning in the teachers' room about a plane that went down over the Atlantic Ocean the night before. Was that the same plane? I also wrestled with relief that her emotional breakdown was not in fact my fault and that my complicated news about med school would be put to rest, at least for now. "That's just... awful," I whispered, guiding her down on the sofa. "What happened?"

"I don't know the details." She sniffed, wiping her nose with the sleeve of her favorite Plymouth State sweatshirt.

She wrapped her legs around my torso and buried her face into my neck. "I just know… they died."

"I'm so sorry, Tess."

"I… just…" She held me tighter. "Poor Bex."

Bex? No wonder she is upset, I thought to myself. Tessa talked about her job often and spoke about a little boy named Bex many times since the school year began. Tessa had grown quite fond of him and was proud of the work she had done with him since the fall. No wonder her heart was breaking into a million pieces. "It was Bex? Oh, God."

She nodded her head and continued to weep into my shirt collar. "There's more."

"More?"

"Yeah," she mumbled into my neck.

"What is it? Is Bex okay? Oh man, he wasn't on the plane, was he?"

"No," she replied, briskly shaking her head. "Thank God he's okay… in a physical sense, at least." She peered up from beneath her matted hair and tear-streaked face, eyes locked on mine, suddenly very no-nonsense, which was an unusual characteristic for my girlfriend. "It's *me*, Noah."

"What do you mean… it's you?"

Tessa brushed her hair away from her face and squinted her eyes closed, as if doing so would make all of this go away. "It doesn't make any sense!"

You're not making sense, I thought, suddenly allowing my own impatience to get the better of me. "Tessa, I have no idea what you are talking about. Do you think this is somehow your fault?"

She held her hand up as if to say *stop*. "Noah. I got a call today from a woman who claimed to be Bex's great-grandmother," she explained, her voice growing louder in volume but her voice steady. "She is the executor for the estate of Bex's parents."

"Estate?"

"Yes, estate. She's really old and lives somewhere in Maine," she said hastily, as if these details were insignificant. "Like in some kind of retirement home."

"What did she want with *you*?"

Tessa pried herself off my lap, collected her hair on top of her head with one hand, and placed her open hand on her hip. I processed her movements in slow motion, and as she started to explain what had happened, an unexpected pit formed inside my gut, because somehow, I knew, once those words left her lips and were spoken into existence, our lives would never be the same.

"They nominated me. For guardianship of Bex."

"Guardianship?" I asked more loudly than I meant to. I, too, jumped to my feet, and this time, I began pacing around her small living room. "You're kidding, right?"

"You think I would joke about this—"

"Why? There must be an aunt, or another family member…" I said. Then I became completely aware of how insensitive I sounded in the heat of the moment.

"Well, there isn't. Apparently his parents met with an attorney prior to their vacation. They were tying up some loose ends and decided to re-evaluate who they would leave him with if something happened… and it's *me*, Noah. They left him to me."

"This is insane," I gasped.

"Yeah, it is. But it's happening."

"And… and are you considering it?"

"Noah… there isn't anything to consider. Apparently, I'm all he has."

I could feel the blood rush to my cheeks as my heart started to pound faster and faster. The walls of her tiny apartment suddenly closed in around me. What was she thinking? Did she have any idea how this would impact her?

How it would impact us? "You are twenty-three years old. You can't raise a child."

"Excuse me?"

"I'm sorry, I know I sound like an ass… but Tessa, you aren't even his family."

Her eyes narrowed, and for a moment I wished I could take that last comment back. "Family?"

"You know what I mean—"

Tessa's cheeks turned crimson as she crossed her arms over her chest, eyes wide. "Oh, like *we're* family?" she shouted, holding up her left hand and pointing at her naked ring finger.

"Tess—"

"Don't," she shouted. "I'm doing this, Noah… with or without you and the insanely gorgeous, twisted halo platinum emerald cut engagement ring that you are hiding in the glove compartment of your jeep. Because right now, Noah…" She paused for a beat. "Bex is more family to me than you are… because at least I know with one hundred percent of my entire being that *he* needs me. But you know what, Noah? I'm just not so sure if you do anymore."

IN THE FUTURE

WRITER SALT PODCAST WITH SEAN ANDERSON

Sean: I don't know, man. Hearing that story just *never* gets easier.

Cassidy: Tell me about it. I just can't even begin to imagine what that was like for you, Tessa... and of course... poor Bex... Such a tragedy.

Tessa: Yeah. It was so long ago now, but I remember it like it was yesterday. I got the call in the middle of my lunch break. It was Bex's great-grandmother, and she was sobbing uncontrollably. She explained what happened... the plane crash... all of it, and she informed me that I was nominated as guardian... She didn't ask if I ·would do it... It was just assumed that I would.

Sean: That must have felt so surreal.

Tessa: Surreal is an understatement. I was shocked... I had a hard time believing it at first.

Sean: Tell us what it was like, making the decision to care for Bex.

Tessa: There was really nothing to decide. I knew it was the right thing to do.

Sean: And Noah didn't feel the same way.

Cassidy: *(chuckles)*

Tessa: No, he didn't. *(sighs)* But in his defense, he did try. At first, he freaked out and didn't want me taking on the responsibility, but then he came around. He decided that he would stick by me, help me raise Bex. But then… he came to the funeral for Mr. and Mrs. Allen… and just fell apart. My court date came up for guardianship, and he just didn't show up. I had assumed that it was just all too sad for him… that he had given up.

Sean: And that's when you went into the city to live with your parents?

Tessa: Yes. I didn't sign my school contract for the next year, and I went to Boston to live with my mom and dad.

Cassidy: And Noah?

Tessa: Ironically, Noah also left Plymouth for Boston… He started med school that fall, and we just sort of lost touch.

Sean: That must have been awful… considering…

Tessa: Considering he was the love of my life?

Sean: Exactly.

Cassidy: It's heartbreaking.

Tessa: It had been devastating. Noah was my whole life… my world… but Bex…

Sean: Bex needed you more.

Tessa: Yup.

Sean: So, the year was 2016 when this all went down. Bex was in first grade?

Tessa: Yes. He was six years old when… *(pauses)* when they died.

Sean: And you picked up, moved to Boston, and started a new life.

Tessa: Yes. We found a private elementary school for Bex in the city. They were amazing… It was truly the perfect fit for him.

Sean: And your career?

Tessa: Thanks to my mom and dad, I was able to take a couple of years to figure things out. I tied up some loose ends with my certifications and was eventually able to start in a private practice in Massachusetts part-time. Having fewer hours was helpful, especially considering the extra interventions and grief counseling that Bex had to undergo. I was able to move out of their place when Bex turned ten. But it was *hard.* Bex's tuition and the rent on my condo were not cheap, and I wasn't able to work part-time anymore. The life insurance money was helpful, but I was determined to save that for Bex. I was a very young single parent, and trying to balance my career with being there one hundred percent for him was just… the hardest thing. I was in a dark place. So much so I was starting to worry about my own mental health.

Cassidy: *(interrupts)* I can't even imagine. I'm so glad things turned around when they did.

Tessa: *(laughs)* You and me both!

Sean: Talk us through it, Tess. When did things start to turn around?

Tessa: Well, it all started with a school essay, believe it or not. Bex wrote an essay on how much he missed his *real* parents, and from that day forward…*(pauses)* Well, I guess you could say from that day forward, our lives were forever changed.

IN THE PRESENT

TESSA

June 2022

Sometimes I get so caught off guard by the choices I have made that it takes my breath away. I continuously struggle with processing just how quickly my life changed course in the blink of an eye. Consequences that came about because of decisions that seemed simple and harmless but in the big scheme of things were life-changing and monumental. For example, Samantha and David Allen made the decision to go on vacation. They *chose* their airline and their departure time with the click of a button and an online payment. I'm sure those decisions seemed like minor details at the time. They may have considered a direct flight versus a layover somewhere, thinking that maybe there was less of a chance of luggage lost on a direct flight. Or maybe they chose their airline based on which one had the best food accommodations. None of that matters now, because they didn't make the right decision when it came to their plane.

Then they *chose* to leave their only son to me, and I, in turn, agreed to raise him once they were gone. I prayed every day for the past six years that it was the right decision, for Bex's sake.

And now, as I stare out the subway window, riding the blue line with Bex from downtown to East Boston, just as I do every afternoon, I study his fingers as they tap away on his phone as he plays a game of some sort. Darkness screams through the window of the lightless underground tunnel. I can't help but wonder—when we are forced into making a choice and we make it, does it then become impossible to live with the consequences... even if it was the right choice and the best option? At what point is it easier to be told what to do? I find that it is sometimes much easier to blame someone when things go wrong. But what if there is no one to blame?

Of course, taking care of him was the only choice. His great grandmother made it clear that there was simply nobody else. Samantha Allen's parents had divorced when she was only a child. Her father left them to start a completely new life with another family. Her mother then passed away suddenly when Samantha was a freshman in high school. Mr. Allen had been estranged from his family. I hadn't learned the details, but Bex's great grandmother did inform me that if the changes were not made to the estate prior to the flight overseas, Mr. Allen's sister would have been the nominee for guardianship. I was not privy to any more information, but according to the State of New Hampshire, I was the best fit for guardianship based on the plan that the Allen family had put in motion. I never truly understood why they chose me, but did it matter anyway? I was granted guardianship over Bex, and by the time he was eight years old, I had officially adopted him. Beckett Allen was my son, and I wouldn't have it any other way.

I tap Bex gently on the knee and motion for him to remove his AirPod from his ear. "Did you have a good day today, Little Monkey?" I ask, like I do every day.

He smiles and nods, and his boyish grin and mysterious brown eyes melt my heart. He runs his fingers through his shaggy brown hair. "It was good, but math was hard again."

I nod, thinking about this for a beat. Academics had always come easy for my son, but something about middle school just changed *everything*. Even with his 504 in place and the necessary accommodations, Bex was starting to struggle with his higher-level areas of study. "What are you working on? Maybe I can help."

"Percents and fractions," he mumbles, making a sour face, like he has eaten something disgusting.

"I can help with that," I reassure him. "I'm great at percents."

"You are?"

"Yes. I have a lot of tricks up my sleeve."

"You do?"

"Yup."

"Maybe we can do it later? I made it to level six," he said, motioning to his phone.

"Think of it this way," I begin, ignoring his request. "If you study super hard for a spelling test and you get an A+, then you probably got a one hundred percent, right?"

"Yes."

"Yeah, so you got all of them right. If there are one hundred questions on a spelling test and you only get fifty of them right, that's a fifty percent."

"That's an F," he says, chuckling. "That's *not* a good grade."

"It's not," I agree. "Also, do you know how many pennies are in a dollar?"

"One hundred."

Bex fidgets with his phone, and I can tell he's eager to get back to his game. I place my hand gently on the back of his neck. "Stay with me," I encourage. "So, ten of those pennies out of one hundred would then be..." I pause for a beat, knowing that my little tutorial is enough for Bex to grasp this mathematical concept.

"Ten percent," he says, satisfied with himself.

"Correct!"

He nods and sticks his AirPod back in his ear. I wrap my arm around his shoulder and smile, thankful that this kind of affection is still acceptable on the subway, given he is well into the tween years. Bex leans his head on my shoulder, and for a moment, my exhaustion begins to dissipate. "I love you, Little Monkey," I whisper.

He takes out one headphone and peers up at me with the sweetest smile, and my heart all but melts. "I love you too, Mom. With one hundred percent of my heart."

* * *

BY THE TIME I put Bex to bed, clean up from dinner, and start making lunches for tomorrow, it is well past 10:00 p.m. I am in desperate need of a shower, since I am pretty sure the amount of dry shampoo I have lathered into my messy bun over the past few days exceeds the recommended dosage, but the idea of bathing tonight all but puts me over the edge. Although I love nothing more than ripping off my work clothes and slipping on my favorite leggings and oversized T-shirt, I have been on autopilot for far too long, and unfortunately, I lost the luxury of feeling comfortable and taking care of myself a long time ago.

I finish cutting the crust off Bex's cheese sandwich, look around for a paper towel, and realize that the roll is once again empty. Wincing, I wipe my hands on my black dress pants, groaning with frustration as I realize Bex has left his lunchbox in his backpack once again. I hustle over to the entryway of our two-bedroom condo and locate his belongings. I find his red-and-black Nike lunchbox and remove it from his bag. At the last minute, I decide to double-check his folder for any unfinished homework or completed assignments... and then I see it—the essay.

I have always adored his handwriting, but now, the carefully formed letters seem to scream off the college-ruled paper in blue ink and shame me in all the wrong ways. "Why I Miss My Real Parents" by Beckett Walker. For a moment, my heart stops beating. Bex and I have spent years working through his grief, and I always encouraged him to talk to me about his birth parents. So why, now, is this such a shock? Why do these two stapled pages make me want to curl up in a ball on the floor and cry, or run into my bedroom and scream into my pillow? How, six years later, do I still somehow feel as if the death of his parents is my fault? I plop down on the entryway floor and curl up against the wall, my fingers shaking and my knee bouncing involuntarily as I force myself to read my son's assignment, an assignment I'm pretty sure should have been worthy of a phone call home from the teacher to me... his *mother*.

Why I Miss My Real Parents
by Beckett Walker

WHEN I WAS A LITTLE KID, I had two different parents than I have now. I had a mom and a dad. My dad worked a lot, but my mom was home every day. She used to make me cheese sandwiches and put notes in my lunchbox. She always wrote "I love you, Little Guy" on the notes. I didn't like to be away from her when I was at school, and the notes helped a lot.

My real parents died in a plane crash. They left for

TEN PERCENT OF MY HEART

Europe, and they never came back. For a long time, I thought this happened to everyone. Like, you start your life with one set of parents and then get new ones later... but this hasn't happened to my friends. Some of my friends' parents are divorced. Some of my friends only have a mom or a dad, but none of them have parents that died in a plane crash. I'm happy for them because it really sucks.

I'm scared that I'm forgetting my real parents. My birth mother was beautiful, like a movie star or a model, even. She was taller than my dad, and I think that scared him a little. Everyone that she met really liked her. My father was a business guy and had an important job. He wore a suit to work every day, and even though he was busy he would always kiss me goodnight before he went to sleep.

My favorite memory of my real parents is when they brought me to a place with a big lighthouse and a huge beach. I don't remember the name of it, but it was cool. There was an arcade there, and we won a ton of tickets. I traded them in for bags of candy and a kite. I remember my parents being happy there too. I don't like to go in the water, but I really like to look at it. I don't like the sand and the way it feels when it gets in between my toes, or even worse, in my bathing suit, but I really liked being there with them. If I had one wish in the whole entire world, it would be to have one more day at that lighthouse with my real parents.

My birth parents loved my new mom so much that they gave me to her. My mom is pretty, too, and very nice. When I was in first grade, she used to make me feel better by giving me Hershey Kisses and making me laugh. She puts notes in my lunchbox, too, even though I'm getting a little too old for notes (I'm afraid to tell her because it might hurt her feelings). My new mom makes cheese sandwiches, too... and she even cuts the crust off. Sometimes, she even sneaks Hershey

Kisses in my lunchbox. That is why my parents left me with her... because she knows how to make everything better.

My real parents died in a plane crash. I miss them very much. I don't want to forget them... but I'm also running out of ways to remember. By Bex.

I WIPE the tears off my face with the sleeve of my blouse and realize that I hadn't even noticed I was crying. This was the first I had ever heard Bex describe Samantha Allen in this way, or even mention anything about a family vacation to a lighthouse on a beach. I read the essay once again, choking up over certain parts and smiling at others. I place it down beside me on the floor and curl up in a fetal position, and without warning, I begin ugly crying. Like, huge, enormous wails that come from somewhere deep inside that I have not allowed to surface in six years. I press my face into my arm in effort to muffle the obnoxious, monstrous noises that are somehow escaping from my soul. I can't wake up Bex—he can't see me like this.

I have done everything I can do for this child, but I will never be able to bring back Sam and David Allen. I have helped him to grieve in every way I know how, but it just won't be enough. He will always hurt over this, and the thought of that makes my heart hurt more. And what about the grief I have yet to unpack? The love of my life, Noah, ripped away from me in an instant. These wounds that are opening are raw... and although I know they need to be addressed, I just don't have the energy.

I'm not sure how much time has passed when I finally peel my sorry self off the hard, cold floor and make my way to my bedroom. A shower will need to wait until tomorrow. I am just too exhausted to do another thing. I make a mental note to look through some of the boxes that had been sent over from the Allen family's storage, some things that his great-grandmother wanted him to have, things that I probably should have done already. Hell, I probably should have taken him to see her by now... but who really knows how to handle these situations until you are in them? There was no course in undergrad or even my masters' classes that explained how to raise a child whose parents died tragically when you never even really knew them yourself. Maybe something in one of those boxes can help Bex through his grief. But for now, I have nothing left to give. I collapse on top of my cream-colored Sherpa comforter and bury my mascara-dripping face into my satin pillowcase. By the time I realize I'm still in my work clothes, it is too late. I am already drifting to sleep, eager for the one thing I have left —my dreams. A place I can go to and remember when life was easier, a place where I can visit Noah and, even if just for a split second, pretend like everything is going to be okay.

"He said what?" Kayla's high-pitched voice pierces the depths of my entire being through my headphones, making me cringe for a beat.

"Nothing bad," I say, surely in attempt to reassure myself, not just Kayla. "It was just an essay. He's grieving... It's very appropriate, actually."

"Come on, Tess... That must have been awful to read."

I pause for a second to gather my thoughts, continuing meanwhile to sift through the boxes I had pulled down from my closet that afternoon. There are two of them, both labeled Allen in black Sharpie marker. I had shrugged off the guilty thoughts that were ricocheting through my mind, reassuring myself that I was waiting until Bex got older before giving them to him... but I know that isn't true. My own anxiety surrounding Bex and the Allen family has many layers, and it is time to face them.

"So, you're okay with it, then?" Kayla asked. My sister-in-law, Kayla, is not okay unless everyone else is okay, and that is why I love her. She is a phenomenal mother to my niece, Zoe, and a fabulous wife to my brother, Lucas. I haven't been to visit her since college, but she comes into the city when she can, and we talk on the phone almost every day.

"I mean, yes but no," I admit, trying to be as honest as I can. "I'm happy he is expressing himself. That's all I can ask for, right?" I study the stack of books I have removed from the first box, and a feeling of melancholy washes over me. "Children's books," I whimper, wiping away an uninvited tear.

"Huh?"

"The first box. It contains children's books... I'm assuming these are the books Sam used to read to Bex."

Kayla is silent for a moment until muttering, "Oh, Tess... are you sure it's a good time to open the boxes? I'm worried about you."

I nod, like she can see me, and flip through the book's dusty covers, painfully aware of how special they once were to Samantha Allen and her son: *The Brave Little Toaster, The Little Engine That Could, Guess How Much I Love You, Where the Sidewalk Ends*. "It's important. He needs to grieve his parents. Besides, it's not me you need to worry about, it's your nephew, Beckett." But even as I say these words, I am overwhelmed with so many unexpected emotions that I decide I need to move on to the next box. I peek at my Apple Watch and remember that I must leave in fifteen minutes to get Bex, who has been at the park with his friends. "I'm opening the other box."

"Okay. Man, I need a glass of wine, and I'm not even you."

"Tell me about it," I agree, ripping open the second box to

discover that this one is filled with what seem to be thick photo albums and scrapbooks. "Pictures," I sigh. "Looks like some scrapbooks and photo albums." I flip through the pages, blowing off the dust and rubbing the tip of my itchy nose with my index finger. I poke through quickly, although I could sit here for the entire day, studying each photograph, because Kayla and I have a mission: to figure out which lighthouse Bex is referring to in his essay. It sounds an awful lot like York Beach, Maine... the place I grew up and where Kayla currently resides with my brother, Lucas. Sure enough, about three quarters of the way into the second scrapbook... I see it. Bex looks to be about five years old, and I realize with sadness that the photo was probably taken that last summer they were together. In one photo, Bex is perched on a rock in front of the Nubble Lighthouse with a gigantic drippy chocolate ice-cream cone. In another, he is in the same spot, this time perched on the laps of Samantha and David. "We were right."

"What?" Kayla asks, clearly between bites of her lunch.

"It's the Nubble. He was writing about the Nubble."

"Holy shit."

"Yeah."

"Our Nubble?"

"Our Nubble." I shake my head and rub my fingers over my tired eyes. "The day I met with her... she noticed the photo of Noah and me in front of the lighthouse, in the same exact spot."

"Did she say anything about it?"

"The photo?"

"Yes."

"Yeah, actually. She asked about it, and I told her that it was a special spot for my family. I explained that I grew up in York... I guess I hadn't thought anything of it."

"What's her last name?"

"It was Allen," I answered, shuddering at the finality of the word *was*.

"No, I mean her maiden name."

"I… I don't know," I say, a bit embarrassed that I don't have this information. "But I'll tell you what, Kayla, I'm going to find out. But I've got to go get Bex."

"Okay," she says, her words muffled from the food she is eating. "But Tessa?"

"Yeah?"

"I think it's finally time you get your butt back here. You know we would love to have you."

"I know," I sigh, realizing that she is right. The only time I had spent with my brother and his family was over the holidays at my parents' home in Boston. I wanted to visit Lucas and Kayla; I just hadn't been able to get out of my own way. "School is out for the summer soon. I'll keep you posted."

"Yes!" she shrieks, overjoyed. "I can't wait to tell Lucas and Zoe."

"Just… just keep it between us for now. I need to figure out what this means for work."

"Of course," she agrees. "But keep me posted. I'm *dying* to see you."

IN THE PRESENT

TESSA

June 2022

The Anderson Cottage. I had read about it in a series of novels written by Sean Anderson, a local author. The books came highly recommended by Kayla and Lucas, since Sean conducted numerous writing workshops at the high school where Lucas teaches language arts. Although I had read about the cottage in a fictional context and remembered it from my childhood, I had never actually had the opportunity to see the inside of it until now.

When I informed Lucas that I was coming home to York for a couple of weeks, he was beyond excited. He had insisted I stay with him, Kayla, and Zoe. But in truth, I have gotten so used to being independent with Bex that I feel I need space. Besides, this is not simply a trip for pure enjoyment. This is, in fact, a grief journey for my son, and I am sure he will be needing his space at times, just as I know I will.

Lucas suggested we rent at the Anderson Cottage. The

second and first floor are being occupied for the entire summer, but Lucas discovered that although it is not publicly listed for rent, the third floor is available. Sean Anderson (the guy who writes the books) lives with his wife, Cassidy, on the second floor, and the first floor has been rented out through the end of August.

I have managed to take a leave of absence from work, deciding to keep on a couple of clients through telehealth. It is not the most beneficial move for my career, but my job is not the most important thing anymore. When I approached Bex about the essay, he was defensive at first. "They made me write about something sad," he shrilled, his voice louder than normal. "I had nothing else to write about, Mom."

"You don't have to apologize," I reassured him. "It's a great essay, and I'm proud of you." But I couldn't ignore the intensity of the emotions that shot at me through those dark eyes. My poor little guy was remorseful for sharing his feelings. "Hey," I had said, overly cheerful. "I have the best news. We are spending a couple of weeks with Uncle Lucas and Aunt Kayla. And guess what, that lighthouse you talked about in your essay? We are going to visit."

"For real?"

"For real."

"Will Zoe be there?"

"Of course." I chuckled. "She can't wait to see you."

"Do I have to go swimming?" he asked, his voice serious and his brow furrowed.

"No, Bex. You don't have to go swimming."

He breathed a deep sigh of relief. "Do you think they still have chocolate ice cream?"

"I'm willing to bet they do, buddy."

That had been two weeks ago to the day. And now, as I unpack a Keurig machine and my favorite mugs from my last box, I breathe a sigh of relief. *I did it,* I think. *We are home.* The kitchen is small but the perfect size for just Bex and me. Kayla had informed me that the third floor was recently remodeled by Sean and Cassidy Anderson. I assume she is referring to the white subway tile backsplash and granite countertop, since they are surprisingly more modern than I had expected. The custom-made cabinets and hardwood floor still smell like new construction, one of my favorite scents. In the corner of the room sits a small table for four. I recall a bit of content from Sean's book and realize this is where his character Emiline Wilson would sit with her parents during teatime. If his stories are true, this is also where Emiline would vacation with her family years later. I make a mental note to pick Sean's brain about his stories. I need to know how much of them are fact and how much are fiction.

I stare out the large windows over the kitchen sink and admire the Atlantic from Long Sands Beach. I hadn't realized how much I had missed this place until now. It is low tide, and the water seems to extend farther out than my eyes can perceive. It is crowded for June, but the weather is beautiful. It is nearing dinner time, and I can almost start to see the sun showing evidence of an emerging sunset. Magnificent lavender and pink wispy clouds cover the hazy blue sky like watercolor brushstrokes, and within seconds I feel the muscles in my neck and shoulders begin to relax.

I glance down at my phone, checking to see if Lucas or Kayla have texted. We have plans to meet up first thing tomorrow on Short Sands Beach. I have yet to inform Bex of this, and I am anticipating his disappointment, since he has made me perfectly aware of his feelings regarding beach sand. Bex is unpacking in his bedroom, and I decide to take a moment for myself... a thought that hasn't crossed my mind in what feels like years. I make myself a coffee in my favorite mug, carefully add and stir in a tablespoon of almond milk, and head onto the deck. I am a bit starstruck in a sense over Sean Anderson, so I silently wonder if Sean and Cassidy are home. I've always been a person who gets nervous around anyone with any sort of celebrity status. I once tried to sneak backstage with Noah at a One Direction concert, determined to meet the band. Although Noah worked his charm with the security guards, we were very nicely escorted outside, but we did not leave empty-handed. They sent us packing with two One Direction bumper stickers and generic autographed postcards.

Noah. Although I keep his spirit with me like an imaginary friend, a secret make-believe companion, I hadn't had the time to really stop and think about the real him for ages. But now, as I sit on the porch on the third floor of the Anderson Cottage, coffee in hand, beach breeze in my hair, I can't help myself. I log into my Instagram account and notice that it has been so long since I did this that I need to re-enter my password. After I do, I cringe at how outdated my profile picture is. It is a selfie that I took at my college friend's wedding. My dark hair was in an updo with a few curly strands hanging down. If I remember correctly, that was about a year after… after Bex. I continue swiping through my phone and type Noah's name in the search window. Sure enough, his very public account appears on my device, and I regret it instantly. There, smiling back at me in numerous Instagram photos, is my ex-boyfriend. Although he is six years older, he looks just as good, if not better, than he did. His smile taunts me from his profile picture, and so do his perfect hair and perfect teeth. His username is Noah_Clark_91 followed by #NoahclarkMD, and his profile reads Doctor of Internal Medicine, Boston MA.

"Noah," I whisper out loud to myself. I trace his face with my pointer finger, and my heart aches deeply. I make the mistake of clicking on his Instagram posts, only to realize that Noah Clark MD is no longer single but very much taken. Taken by a female who looks way younger than him and besides that... way prettier than me. "She looks like freaking Barbie," I moan, louder than I mean to. I close Instagram, put my phone face down on the table, wrap my fingers around my steamy hot mug, sip my coffee, and close my eyes... something I do to quiet the noise. It can be awkward at times, but I find that closing my eyes can be my way of escaping, even if only for a minute. I listen to the silence and allow the peaceful and familiar salt air to encompass me, and for a brief second, I'm able to put the vision of Noah out of my mind. That is, until I need to pick my phone back up again and check out his girlfriend, or whoever she is, one more time.

* * *

I POP OPEN the trunk of my silver Honda Civic and begin unloading our beach gear. Packing up had taken me half an hour longer than I had expected, and just when I thought I was set, the gear didn't all fit into my car. I knew my brother was going to give me a hard time for overpacking, but this is my first trip to the beach in years, and keeping Bex comfortable means there are things we just can't live without. I had done extensive research in this area, and after consulting both Google and the occupational therapist at Bex's school, we came up with a list of items that would help him enjoy the beach regardless of his sensory issues. A popup tent, water shoes, beach blanket, socks, an extra bathing suit, a compression sun shirt, a bucket hat, and sunglasses, to name a few.

I grab my oversized cooler by the handles and set it down next to Bex's feet just in time to see my niece, Zoe, galloping up the sandy hill towards our car in a purple two-piece bathing suit. *When the heck did she grow up?* I think, realizing that the last time I saw Zoe, she looked more like a child and less like a teenager. I quickly do the math in my mind and realize that although she is a couple of years younger than Bex, she looks like she could pass for thirteen. "Auntie!" she shrieks. "Bex! Auntie TJ! You're here!" I smile, finding my nickname comforting in ways I hadn't expected. My full name, Tessa Jean, was abbreviated by my brother to TJ when we were kids. I hadn't realized how much I missed hearing it until now.

"It's so good to see you!" I tell Zoe. I scoop her up into my arms and kiss her on top of her head. "I love your braid," I remark, running my fingers over her brunette tresses. "You look so grown-up, Zoe."

She blushes and turns toward Bex. "Hi, Bex," she sings cheerfully. She leans toward him, hoping for a hug, but he takes a step back. I pause, waiting to see if he can use one of the strategies we have been working on. Sure enough, he extends his fist out to Zoe for a fist bump and says in his coolest and most chill voice possible, "What's up, Zoe."

She returns the fist bump and jumps up and down. "The waves are huge," she exclaims as Bex frowns and takes another step toward me.

"I'm sure they are!" I reply. "Can you grab your parents? We could use some help with all of this stuff…"

As if on cue, Lucas and Kayla approach our car hand in hand. Lucas hasn't changed a bit. His chestnut-colored hair glistens in the sun as he walks toward me shirtless. "Teeeee-jjj," he calls in his goofiest brotherly tone. "Get over here!" I reach up to hug my brother, who is way taller than I am, but without missing a beat, he is picking me up and shaking me from side to side. "I missed you, sis," he says, dropping me back to the ground.

"I missed you too," I say.

"There's my guy!" he exclaims, reaching down toward Bex and high-fiving him. Lucas places his hand on the sleeve of Bex's long-sleeved white swim shirt. "Great to see you, Bex."

"Great to see you too, Uncle Lucas."

"You're really here!" Kayla shrieks.

"We are!"

"Come here!" she demands, pulling me close. Her dark hair is pulled into two low pigtails tucked beneath a baseball cap that reads Mom Life. I reach up and hug my sister-in-law, and my heart rages with happiness. Because for the first time in a long while, I feel like I am finally where I need to be—home.

Sure enough, my big brother cracks a few jokes about the number of unnecessary belongings I have in tow, and we work together to lug all of them from my car and down the sandy hill to our spot on Short Sands Beach. It is high tide, which doesn't leave much shore, but Lucas and Kayla have set up their gear in a spot with just enough room for Bex and me to join. "The tide will go down soon," Lucas explains to Bex, who looks like he might throw up at the sight of the massive, dark swells that are forming and collapsing not too far from us.

"The sand is hot," Bex mutters out of the corner of his mouth.

I peer down at his feet and realize that even though he is wearing Crocs, the sweltering beach sand has seeped into his shoes. "Give me a minute," I say. "Let me set up and then I can help you."

"But it's hot," he says, more loudly this time.

I move as quickly as I can, tossing the beach blanket down on the sand and instructing him to stand on it. He does, and for a moment his anxiety seems to decrease. "What can I do?" Kayla asks, completely aware of my own anxiety regarding

Bex's. I shrug because I don't even know what *I* can do. "Want me to set up your tent?" she asks.

"Yes, that would be helpful."

Kayla and Lucas begin working on the tent, and I gesture for Bex to take a seat in one of the chairs. He does, but just by looking at him for a moment, I can sense that he is underwhelmed by the beach scene and probably regretting writing that essay more and more every second. "You okay?" I ask, knowing very well that he is not.

"Meh," he replies... one of my favorite Bex responses.

"Just hang tight," I encourage. "Once we get set up, you will be good."

"Do you need sunblock?" Kayla asks.

"We did it before we left," I explain, recalling how much Bex hated applying sunblock. "Bex, do you think you want your water shoes?"

He shrugs, eyes wide, and I can tell he is trying hard to keep it together. "Let's try them," I suggest. "If you don't like them, we can take them off."

I grab a towel and wipe the sand off my son's feet. He chuckles for a moment as I help him slide on his water shoes. "There," I say. "Better already."

"Auntie TJ, can we go boogie boarding now?" Zoe asks, eyes wide. "Bex, the water is *so* fun. You are going to love it."

"I don't go swimming," Bex explains. "I don't like it."

Zoe nods, the disappointment not going unnoticed. "I'll go with you, kiddo," Lucas chimes in. "You ladies good?" he asks Kayla.

"We've got it," Kayla replies, kissing him on the cheek.

Zoe grabs her boogie board and gives her father the other. "I'll race you!" she challenges. They dart toward the roaring sea, and for a moment I wonder what it would be like to do that with Bex. I imagine what it would be like to see my son let loose and bolt toward that water, just as I did when I was his age.

"Can I have my phone, Mom?" Bex asks. He peeks up at me from under his bucket hat and sunglasses. My heart sinks for a moment because he looks completely miserable.

Feeling defeated, I reach into my beach bag and retrieve Bex's phone, my heart breaking for him as he scoops it up and heads into his beach tent, disappearing from my sight.

"Is he okay?" Kayla whispers from the chair next to me.

"He just needs to adjust," I say, realizing that I'm not sure if I am trying to reassure Kayla or myself.

"Of course," she says.

"The weather is perfect," I say, in an effort to change the subject. I lift my maroon coverup over my head, toss it into my beach bag, and adjust my black bikini top with my free hand. "It really is good to be here."

"Have you gotten to meet Sean and Cassidy?"

"No, not yet. So far, the only sign of life at the Anderson Cottage has been a couple of different girls from the first floor doing the walk of shame. Whoever is staying there is most definitely playing the field."

"Speaking of playing the field," Kayla starts, "I have so many people that you need to meet—"

I hold my hand up in front of my face and stop her midsentence, since Kayla is always working to set people up. Of course, she is often successful, but that is beside the point. "I'm not dating right now," I say, like a parent scolding a child.

"Of course," she starts but stops. She starts again. "But Tessa, have you dated *anyone* since... you know?"

"Since Noah?"

She bites her lip and tilts her sunglasses down, her eyes meeting mine. "Yeah," she says. "Since Noah."

My silence speaks volumes, and I know for a fact she is doing the math in her mind. "Tessa, it's been years…"

"Six years," I finish for her, turning my gaze toward the water.

"Six years! Tessa, that's insane. You're almost thirty years old… You aren't dead."

I put my finger up over my lips and motion to the tent behind us. "I'm pretty sure Bex can hear us," I whisper.

"Sorry," she whispers back. "But Tess, you need to put yourself out there. Human beings… we are wired to share our lives with other people. I hate the idea of you being alone."

"I'm not alone," I say, my shoulders stiffening. "I have Bex."

"Tessa… all I'm saying—"

"Kayla—"

"I miss seeing you smile, hon—"

"Drop it," I beg. "Please?"

"Okay."

"Thank you." I reach into my beach bag and pull out my own cell phone, finding myself on Instagram before I even mean to be. "He's on Insta," I explain, pointing at the phone screen.

"Noah?"

"Yeah, Noah," I say, presenting her with the fakest smile ever.

Kayla scoots over toward me, and I show her his Instagram profile and his long-legged, size-zero blond girlfriend. "Holy shit," she mumbles. "That's Noah's girlfriend?"

"Yup," I say with a sigh. I click on his profile picture, and a photo appears, surrounded by hashtags and @ symbols. "I don't know much about Instagram, but I do know that Noah is hashtag very happy."

"OMG, Tessa… you really *don't* know a lot about Instagram, do you?"

"Why are you making that face?" I ask, confused, as her eyes grow wide and her mouth gapes open.

"You just watched his story."

"His what?"

"His story. He can *see* you."

"He can see me?" I shriek, turning my phone upside down, mortified.

"No," she says, belly laughing. "He can see that you viewed it."

A pit forms in my gut. For a moment, I feel sick. "I'm such an idiot."

"You aren't an idiot, Tessa—"

"Well, when it comes to guys, dating, and Instagram, I am. So if you don't mind, I'd like to just focus on what I came here to do. Show my son a good time, help him remember his birth parents, and continue with my new life."

"Your new life?"

"Yeah," I reply, a little more firmly than I mean to. "One that isn't so much about me, connecting with other humans, and smiling… but about the little boy who is hiding away in that tent."

Kayla places her hand on my arm. "Okay. I'm sorry. I'm here for you."

"Thank you," I say, standing up from my chair and kicking through the sand toward Bex's tent. I duck under the covering and pretend to knock. "Anyone home?" I sing.

"Hi, Mom," Bex replies. He is lying on the tent's floor on his belly, fingers tapping away on the phone screen.

"Hi, Little Monkey. Got room for one more?"

He nods, and I wipe my feet off on a spare towel. I bend down next to him and place my hand on the small of his back. He smells like sunblock and beach air... two very unusual scents for my Bex. "You good?"

"I'm good," he says confidently. "Want to watch me play? It's bike tricks."

"I would love to watch you play," I say, sliding down next to him on my own belly, and glance at his phone.

"Are you trying to get me to go swimming?" he asks, not removing his eyes from the screen.

"Nope. But I was thinking that maybe later we can go find that chocolate ice cream?"

The corners of his mouth turn up into a half smile, and although he doesn't peel his eyes off the game, I know I have his attention. "Okay," he says softly. "But for now, let's just stay here... you and me."

I rest my head on his shoulder and study him as he taps his fingers briskly on the phone screen. "Sounds perfect."

"Really? Because you can go swimming if you want to."

"Really. This is just what I need." I rest the side of my face on my hands like a pillow and close my eyes. I allow the earth's warmness to heat my body and Bex's sweet smile to reassure my soul. I have no doubt that being here with my son in this moment is truly just what I need, and my heart begins to flood with happiness because I am right where I belong.

IN THE PRESENT

TESSA

June 2022

Two days have passed since we settled in at the Anderson Cottage. Although Bex absolutely hates the beach, we have worked together to try to find activities that he can appreciate. So far, we have spent multiple days at the arcade on Short Sands Beach and visited York Animal Kingdom. Bex and Zoe loved seeing the animals and spent hours riding the Ferris wheel. We have planned this evening to go to the Nubble Lighthouse with Lucas, Kayla, Zoe, and some friends of theirs. That isn't until this evening, so Bex and I have the entire day for ourselves. We decide to check out some shops on Long Sands together, since my parents gave Bex quite a bit of spending money, and he intends to spend every cent.

"Can we go in here?" he asks.

We haven't made it very far since our departure from the Anderson Cottage. We are standing in front of a surf shop. A large multicolored sign in the shape of a surfboard reads Sandy Toes Surf Inc.

"It's a surf shop," I explain to him, chuckling at the irony of the situation.

"So?"

"So?" I repeat, adjusting my ponytail and placing my hands on my hips. "The name of the store, it represents everything you have been against."

"You're funny. We can at least check it out."

"Whatever you say, Little Monkey."

Bex opens the door to the surf shop, and I follow closely behind, still curious about why on earth my son would be even slightly interested in a surf shop. As we enter, two men brush past us in wet suits, most likely eager to catch some waves, something I often did when I was younger. I shove away the sudden urge to be out in the open waters, and I stay close behind Bex as he enters the store and begins to browse through T-shirts, sunglasses, hats, and boogie boards. "See anything you like?" I ask him, pausing to try on a pair of sunglasses.

Bex ignores me and continues shopping. I study my reflection in the mirror for a beat and notice that although it's only been a couple of days, I am already seeing a difference in my appearance. My typical business attire has been replaced with a pair of denim shorts and a white spaghetti-strapped tank top. My usual pale skin appears sun-kissed, the dark circles that had become a permanent part of my face have disappeared, and for a moment, I don't recognize myself.

My thoughts are interrupted by a voice coming from the front of the store. "Hey, little dude, can I help you find anything?" I assume that this person must be talking to Bex. I stick the sunglasses back on the rack and bolt over to the front desk, where Bex is apparently making friends.

"He's just looking," I say, more firmly than I mean to. My eyes are glued to Bex, who is holding up a bright-green-and-teal boogie board. He is admiring it like a piece of long-lost treasure.

"I like this one," he says. His eyes grow wide, and he gives me a toothy smile. "Can we get it, *please?*"

"The kid has good taste," the cashier admits.

I give a side glance to the person behind the counter and show them my best *stay out of it* face. "We aren't shopping for boogie boards," I explain to them both, like a teacher addressing a class.

"Why not?" they ask in unison.

I shrug off the stranger behind the counter and turn to my son. "Bex," I explain, my voice growing louder by the second, "you don't *go* in the ocean. Why would *you* need a boogie board?"

"Don't go in the ocean?" the cashier asks. "Who doesn't like the ocean?"

I ignore him once again and bend down so that my eyes are in line with my son's. "Bex, buddy... why do you want a boogie board—"

"Who wouldn't want a boogie board? You're at the beach, dude!"

I feel the blood rush to my cheeks, and I clinch my fists by my sides. *Who does this guy think he is?* "Bex," I instruct. "Go over there and look at the hats. Mom needs to talk to the *boy* behind the counter."

Bex pouts, hands me the boogie board, and storms away. I march back over to the counter, ready to give the person behind it a piece of my mind. "Listen," I say, as calmly as I can. "My son... he doesn't like the ocean... or the beach for that matter. I would appreciate it if you would just let me handle this with him."

"Has he ever been in the ocean?"

"No... yes... well, not really."

"Then how do you know if he likes it or not? Hell, how does *he* know?"

I clinch my fists by my sides and take a deep breath, determined not to let whoever this guy is get the best of me. I close my eyes and channel my inner mama bear. "Because," I hiss, "he has a diagnosis of sensory integration and modulation disorder... and the beach, it, well, it drives him nuts.... not as much as you are driving *me* nuts right now, mind you ...but my son... he likes the idea of swimming, but he doesn't want to swim. It's been a *long* couple of days here... and I would just appreciate it if you would.... well, if you could just let us be."

"Okay."

I realize that I haven't even looked up at this person yet, and when I do, I am somewhat caught off guard. I'm not sure who exactly I expected to see sitting there, but I didn't expect to see *him*. "Hi," he says, finding humor in my outburst. He is perched on a stool, whoever he is. He wears a pair of short orange swim shorts and a black tank top that reads Sandy Toes Surf. I'm not quite sure what the purpose of the shirt is, because it exposes more of his torso than a shirt should. I blush, embarrassed at how out of control I feel. Years have passed since I last found anyone attractive, but I can't help but study him... like I'm observing a painting at a museum. I am mesmerized by the way the muscles in his chest and his arms seem to be constructed perfectly and molded in ways I've never seen up close. Both biceps are wrapped in tattoos of various uniquely shaped waves of different colors, and for a moment I find this captivating... and annoying, because I had a reason for coming up to this desk, but right now, I seem to have forgotten why. "You were saying?" he asks, obviously mocking me. I try to be angry, but as he smiles at me, I am hypnotized by his eyes. I have never seen eyes this blue before. *This must be the bluest that God makes eyes,* I think. They are intense but at the same time wild and carefree. "Your son? Doesn't like the water? A sensory disorder or some kind... I drive you nuts..." He adjusts his backward baseball cap and rubs his fingers over his chin, looking somewhat amused and maybe a little concerned.

I glance over my shoulder at Bex, who is trying on a pair of sunglasses and checking himself out in the mirror. *Get it together, Tessa*, I silently scold myself. I take a deep breath and stand upright, still holding onto the boogie board. "Yes. He doesn't need a boogie board because he doesn't swim in the ocean."

"Okay," the cashier says. He tilts his head and studies me for a beat.

"Okay?"

"Yeah, okay. But I think you're making a mistake. How do you know you don't like something if you've never tried it in the first place?"

I take two steps backward and start to place the boogie board on the rack, but something stops me. Is it this guy's smile? Is it his eyes? Is it the way he is looking at me? Is it the audacious way he acts like he knows Bex better than I do? Does he not understand how hard I have had to try for the past six years? How far Bex has come? The amount of work that I had to put into coming to the beach? I am so angry with this guy, so why do I suddenly feel the need to stay locked in this spot, in his presence? "Thank you for understanding. We... we will be leaving now."

"I'm Desmond," he says, extending his knuckles out for what I imagine to be an invitation to a fist bump. "Desmond Spencer."

I awkwardly extend my hand out, and we bump fists. "Tessa," I start. Then I stop. "TJ. You can call me TJ."

"I like TJ," he admits, crossing his arms over his chest. My gaze instantly drifts to his tattoos. I've never been attracted to tattoos, but I can't keep my *damn* eyes off them.

"Thanks."

"You can call me Des."

"Des?"

"Yeah. It's spelled D-E-S, but the *S* sounds like a *Z*."

"I like that." I lean the boogie board on the ground against the counter and place my hands in the back pockets of my shorts. "My son," I say, motioning behind me. "His name is Bex, short for Beckett."

"I love that!" Des exclaims. "You can just leave the board on that rack. It doesn't make sense to buy a boogie board if you don't like the ocean," he says loudly enough for Bex to hear him.

"Nope," I say, suddenly letting my guard down. I lean my elbows against the counter, my eyes still locked on his. "He's got a lot going on," I explain.

"I got you," he says, nodding in agreement.

"You *got* me?"

"Yeah, I got you... I've got your back."

"Oh." I chuckle. "Sorry... I didn't get..."

Bex appears by my side.

"You must be Bex!" Desmond exclaims. "My name is Des. I'm a surf instructor here."

I smile, feeling suddenly guilty for my assumptions and very interested in and curious about Des, the surf shop guy. Des and Bex share a fist bump, and the smile on my son's face couldn't be any bigger if he tried. "Des and Bex," I repeat more awkwardly than I mean to. "Very cute."

"Your mom and I were just talking about the boogie board. It doesn't make sense to buy it if you don't like the water."

"Please, Mom! I really want to get it."

I rub my face in my hands, feeling overly frustrated. I

close my eyes and try to process my thoughts. On one hand, I would love for my son to buy this boogie board and body surf his little heart out. On the other, I know it will simply lead to more frustration for him when he tries and just can't handle it. I open my eyes, and my gaze falls on a sign on the wall behind Desmond. Rates and prices for surf camp and surf lessons. "You do lessons?" I ask, my eyes locked on his.

"Yes, ma'am. Surf camp, group, and private lessons."

I perch my elbows on the counter and place my chin in my hands. I bite down on my lower lip and narrow my brows. "I'll buy the board," I say.

"Yeah!" both Bex and Desmond cheer.

I hold my hand up and stop them mid-celebration. "I'll buy the board... on one condition."

"Anything for you, dude," Desmond says, fist bumping Bex once again.

"You let me pay for lessons for Bex... but not for surfing. I need you to get him comfortable in the water. You do that... he can have the boogie board."

Bex suddenly becomes very quiet. Desmond removes his hat, combs his hand through his thick dark tresses, and then sticks it back on his head. He takes a swig from his water bottle and considers this for a second. "Okay," he says. "Deal." He extends his hand out for a handshake, and I receive his hand in mine as I fight off the goofy smile that has started to invade my face. "I'm pretty booked up with camps and lessons... but I'm available during lunchtime... That could work. You guys staying on Long Sands?"

"Anderson Cottage," Bex chimes in. "Third floor."

"Get out of here," Desmond says with a laugh.

"What?" I ask, suddenly confused.

"I live on the first floor. I'm there through the end of August."

I cringe, thinking of the abundance of women who have

been spotted coming and going into the cottage's first floor, and I'm suddenly embarrassed for even silently considering the possibility of... well, of *us*. "Nice," I say, digging through my bag for my wallet, very aware of the blood that has rushed to my cheeks once again. "Okay, Bex, time to go."

"Did I say something wrong?" Desmond asks.

"Nope. Nothing at all," I say, looking him over, wondering for the first time just how old he is. "This is for the lessons and the boogie board," I say, handing him the money. As I do, his fingers graze mine, and my heart flutters unexpectedly.

"Tomorrow at noon?" he asks, opening a binder and adding our names to his schedule.

"Yes... we have something in the morning," I say, recalling the plan we made to meet Bex's great-grandmother at the retirement center for breakfast. "But we will be back at the cottage by noon."

"I'll just come up and grab him, then."

"Grab him?"

"Yeah," he says, chuckling. "For the lesson."

"Oh, *I* will be joining you for the lesson," I insist. "I mean, I can watch from the beach... but I'm just not comfortable—"

"I got you," he says, counting the money and adding it to the cash register.

"Good," I say. "There are some things I do to make him more comfortable... Water shoes might help."

"We'll see about that," Desmond says, winking at me out of the corner of his eye. His lips curl up into a sneaky kind of smile, and although I am still irritated by him in a sense, I can't help but smile back at him, no matter how hard I try.

* * *

"Do you think he will do it? Go in the water?" Kayla asks between bites of her ice cream.

"I would like to think so," I say, licking the bottom of my own ice cream cone, eager to keep the sticky substance from melting onto my fingers. "But this is something I've been working on for a *long* time, and I haven't been successful... and I don't really know much about this guy."

"The surf teacher? The hot one?"

"Yes." I chuckle. "Yes, I guess he is a good-looking guy."

"You guess?"

"Yeah, I mean... for what it's worth... but I wasn't in the store for *me*. I was there with Bex... This is about Bex, not me," I affirm. I stop, allowing myself a moment to process my own words. Of course, these lessons would be about getting Bex comfortable in the ocean. But if that is really where my head is, then why do my knees suddenly feel weak?

"Want to sit there?" Kayla asks, gesturing to a wooden bench that overlooks the Nubble lighthouse. This is one of my favorite spots, and as I stare over the glistening waters of the Atlantic and rest my eyes on the Nubble, a feeling of serenity washes over me. I've always admired how quaint but mighty the lighthouse appears up on its grassy hill. As a child, Lucas and I would beg our parents to take us across the ocean chasm and inside. That would have been trespassing, of course, so instead we settled on drawing pictures of what we thought it might be like.

"Yes," I say. "Do you see the kids?"

"Right down there," she replies, pointing straight ahead and down the rocky ledge. Zoe and Bex are perched on a rock closer to the shore. Bex sits with his legs crossed while Zoe's dangle freely. Both children slurp their ice cream eagerly, and even from a distance I can appreciate the oversized grin that is plastered on my son's face.

"He looks so happy," I say, relief flooding through my veins. "He really likes it here."

"I'm so glad. You both deserve the break."

I smile and nod, becoming mesmerized by the waves and the pattern they create as they crash over the rocky coastline.

"Any more excitement on Instagram?"

"You mean with Noah?"

"Yeah. With Noah."

"Nope," I say, reaching for a napkin and wiping the side of my face. "I think it's pretty obvious he's moved on."

"I feel like that's so fast."

"Kayla," I say with a chuckle. "It's been six years!"

"I know. But I'm not talking about the new girlfriend. I just, I don't know… It was pretty shitty how things went down for you, that's all."

I nod, my gaze jumping from Bex and Zoe and back to the lighthouse. Flocks of seagulls swarm over the head of an elderly man who is feeding the birds. A woman who looks to be the same age as him studies his every motion and looks on… clearly amused by him… clearly… in love? A wave of sadness washes over me. I had often dreamed about Noah and me growing old together. Kayla is right. The way things ended was devastating. At first, he had agreed that raising Bex was the right thing to do… and that we could do it together. He attended Sam and David's funeral… and after that, he was just never the same. He had used medical school as his main reason for leaving, but I knew him well enough to understand that something more was going on… something bigger. "You're right," I admit. "It was a crappy way to end things."

Kayla nudges my arm playfully. "We've got to get you out there."

"Out there?"

"Yes!" she shrieks. "You need to meet someone. I'm great at setting people up. A couple of years ago I set up friends of ours… Hazel and Warren—"

"Kayla! You set them up because you were super jealous, you know… because Hazel was Lucas's ex-girlfriend."

She throws her head back and cringes, placing her ice cream cup on the bench between us. "I forget how well you listen sometimes." Kayla adjusts her baseball cap and pulls her brunette pigtails over her shoulders.

"It's sort of what I do for a living. You know, listen to people. Besides, Lucas is my brother."

"I still set them up," she affirms. "And quite successfully, I might add."

"They got married, right?" I ask, shifting my gaze back to Bex and Zoe, who are now hopping from rock to rock, having the time of their lives.

"Oh yes," she says. "And did I tell you they have a baby on the way?"

"No!" My eyes grow wide as I try to remember how old Hazel is now, if she is the same age as Lucas. "I can't imagine starting over at this point… and I'm twenty-nine."

"Right… She's my age… just about thirty-four."

"Doesn't she have a daughter too?"

"Yes. I can't imagine starting over either. Ellie is a little older than Zoe, which makes her Bex's age… twelve, I believe."

"Well, good for them," I say, genuinely meaning it. Sean Anderson wrote a bit about them in his second book, and I have been silently rooting for Warren and Hazel.

"It will happen for you, Tessa… I just know it."

I run my fingers through my dark tresses and stare out over the open waters. Talking about my own feelings is awkward. I am way more comfortable helping other people solve their problems, not dealing with my own. "Thanks," I say, forcing my best smile. "But like I said… it isn't about me anymore; it just can't be."

"I hear you, Tess. But at some point, you are going to have to make it about you."

I close my eyes and inhale the sweet scent of ocean air and relax the best I can, shutting down the ache that is forming in the pit of my stomach because I know she is right. Noah is moving on, and I should have moved on years ago. But instead of allowing these emotions to take hold of me, I push them away and instead think of a time that was easier, a time when Noah and I were in love. When a simple "I'm sorry" made everything better. I go to that place in my mind and use my imagination, like I often do, to shove away the pain. Noah and I on our first night, the night we met in college. How effortless it had been the first time we were together. The way he ran his fingers through my hair. His lips had felt warm as they kissed my ear, my cheek, my neck. I had often told myself that I knew that night that he was the one. Everything about him just felt right.

"Don't you agree, Tess?" Kayla asks, her soft voice breaking through my daydream.

"About what?"

"You need to get back out there and think about yourself."

"Yes. Someday," I confess. "Someday, Kayla, I will make it about me. But today… just isn't going to be that day."

IN THE PRESENT

NOAH

June 2022

I don't get a ton of time off, so when I do, I am very intentional about how I choose to spend it. Some might say that I overplan, that being so meticulous about every second of my days off isn't healthy. I try to explain that after completing years of medical school and an emotionally and physically taxing residency, I just don't know how to slow down. That is, of course, only half of the truth. Because when I do calm down and force myself to sit with my emotions, I feel like I'm being repeatedly sucker punched in the gut.

Don't get me wrong—things have been going very well for me. The rewards I have experienced for my hard work and my efforts have not gone unnoticed. I graduated my program with honors and in turn was promoted at the hospital straight out of my residency. It turns out that I am good at what I do, and people really like me. My girlfriend,

Nadine, and I have recently become serious. We met in med school and completed our residency together. We started out as friends, but about a year ago things shifted in a different direction. She blames the tequila for our first initial hookup, but I knew that night was more than just too much alcohol consumption, and I hadn't let her off the hook.

So, now, I sit at my favorite coffee shop, on my first day off in what feels like forever, waiting for Nadine to join me. You can imagine my surprise as I mind my own business, flip through Instagram like I might do on any given day, and come across *Tessa Walker's* account. The girl hadn't been on social in years, and *boom*, there she was, viewing my Instagram Story. If I'm being honest, it feels like I've gotten the wind knocked out of me.

I hadn't meant to end things with Tessa the way I did. Regardless of everything that started working against us, I was ready to try. But our relationship just had so many layers, and so much started to change. I loved her so much, and I wanted to make it work... but I just didn't have it in me to go down that road with her. It would have been just too hard in so many ways.

Of course, I've always wished nothing but the best for her. Even after we broke up (one of the worst nights of my entire life), I hoped that we could remain friends. But she was just too busy trying to be a mother, and I was bogged down with med school. I had thought about returning the ring, but I was never able to bring myself to do it. It had been a while since I took it out of my safe, but there was just something inside me, something that couldn't bring myself to return it.

"Hey, cutie!" Nadine sings as she drops her purse on the chair across from me. "Come here often?" She has just come from yoga, and her high-waisted black pants cling to her body in all the right ways, much differently than the scrubs we wear at the hospital.

"*Damn*," I say, pressing my lips together in a whistle. "You look good."

Nadine shakes her head and removes a hair tie from her hair, allowing her long blond tresses to fall freely around her face. "Stop," she says bashfully. She leans forward and kisses me on the cheek. She smells like vanilla and baby powder. I place my hands around her waist and pull her close to me for a better kiss. "Noah," she says, stopping me in the middle of my move. "Noah, not here."

"Sorry," I say, holding my hands up in defeat. "I just can't get enough of you."

"Well, you know how I feel about public displays of affection," she lectures, like a parent correcting a child. "I'm going to order my coffee."

I sip my own coffee and return to my Instagram account. Tessa is no longer "active" on Instagram, and I'm suddenly left feeling kind of blindsided. Surely she must know that I will be able to see that she was looking at my story, right? I briefly consider sending her a direct message but immediately decide against it. Instead, I flip through her old photographs, images that I have seen many times over the years. I pinch my fingers against the screen on my phone and make one of her photos larger. It is a picture of her and Bex, probably right around the time she gained custody of him. I study them, her arms around his shoulders and her face pressed against his. How could this come so naturally to her? If I hadn't known that Bex was Tessa's *adopted* son, I would assume she was his birth mother. Their fair complexions are identical, as are their hair and eye coloring.

I swipe out of Instagram and flip my phone over on the table, rubbing my tired eyes with the palms of my hands. *I can't go down this road*, I think. I made a conscious decision to bail on Tessa and Bex six years ago, and although it was my choice to make, the guilt and shame that came with the consequences of that decision are sometimes impossible to live with.

"Everything okay?" Nadine asks, sliding into the seat across from me and already sipping her latte.

"Yes," I say, smiling at her. "Everything is great." I take her hand in mine and kiss the tips of her fingers, and for a second, as brief as it might be, I believe it myself.

IN THE PRESENT

TESSA

June 2022

"Good morning, welcome to Wells Valley Cove," the doorman says as he holds the door open for Bex and me. Bex enters ahead of me, and I rest my hand on the back of his shoulder, thanking the man who opens the door for us. "Visiting someone today?" he asks.

"Yes," I say, glancing at his silver nametag, which reads Seth Jenson in bold black letters. "This is my son, Bex. We are here to visit with his grandmother, Wendy Jones."

"Right this way," Seth instructs, bumping into me slightly, enough for his arm to brush against mine. I feel the blood rush to my cheeks and scold myself for checking him out. *What's gotten into you, Tessa?* I silently scream. Seth leads us toward a receptionist desk, where I show my ID and sign us in.

"We are meeting her for breakfast," I explain. "I'm assuming that means the dining hall." I glance around and am immediately surprised at how nice this place is. Bex's great-grandmother had explained a little bit about it over the phone, but she hadn't done it justice. Floor-to-ceiling windows welcome in a breathtaking beachfront view, and I can't help but get lost in the sandy stretch of land and the shallow waters of low tide. "This is absolutely beautiful," I say to Seth, motioning to the picturesque scene before me.

Seth cups his hand over the side of his face, bends down closer to me, and whispers, "That's funny... I was just going to say the same about you."

I leap back, completely thrown off guard, and bump into Bex, whose eyes are glued to his phone and who I hope heard none of that. "You okay, Bex?"

"Meh."

I gather my hair onto one of my shoulders and wipe small beads of sweat off my forehead. "Could you... could you please just show me where to go?"

"I'm sorry, is he bothering you?" A woman who appears to be about my age or maybe a bit older is playfully nudging Seth on the arm. Her smile is a friendly one, and I can tell instantly she's got this Seth guy's number and isn't going to let him get away with any of it. She pulls up the sleeves of her black suit coat and reaches forward to shake my hand. "I'm Maggie," she explains. "Maggie Thatcher. I'm an admin here at WVC."

"Tessa Walker." I extend my hand toward hers. "Wow," I say, startled. "That's a beautiful engagement ring." I shake her hand, but my eyes are glued to her ring. Suddenly, Noah's ring and the failed proposal are at the forefront of my mind again.

"I would have gotten her a bigger diamond," Seth boasts as he puts his hands in his pockets and stares up at the ceiling, shaking his head from side to side.

Maggie adjusts her ash-blond hair tighter in her ponytail and rolls her eyes. "Yeah, okay, Seth."

"This is my son, Bex," I say, eager to help her through this moment of obvious discomfort.

"Hi, Bex! I hear you are visiting your great-grandmother today," she says. "I've heard so much about you."

"Hi," Bex says, looking up from his phone for half a second.

"Cassidy told my fiancé, West, that you guys are staying at the Anderson Cottage?"

"Yes, we are," I say, finding it funny how fast word travels in this area. "It's beautiful… and so is this place," I say, admiring the view once more. "I think we are meeting in the dining hall."

"The dining hall? Oh, no. Wendy's got something a little bit better than that up her sleeve."

We begin to head down the hallway, following Maggie as her black Jimmy Choos click-clack against the tile floor. "Like what?" I ask.

"I know a little of your story," Maggie begins. "I know of Bex's situation and that he hasn't seen Wendy for so long that he probably doesn't remember her… Let's just say that we wanted to make this extra special."

"How nice of you," I say. We follow Maggie into a stairwell and hustle down the stairs to keep up with her. She is obviously a woman on a mission. When we exit the building, I am blown away by the scene before me. Not only does it feel like we are at an oceanfront five-star resort stacked with lounge chairs and tables, but we are standing in the middle of several groups of tables and chairs, all set up for breakfast on the beach. "This is adorable," I say, studying the outdoor restaurant-style seating.

"Isn't it?" Maggie agrees. "I came up with the idea for the

outdoor café. The residents hate being cooped up inside all day, and it works out well when they have visitors."

"That's wonderful," I say. My gaze drifts out toward the water, and I notice that even at this early hour, one of the residents is already wading through the tiny waves of low tide.

"That's Art," Maggie says, smiling. "He's actually my fiancé's grandfather."

"How nice," I say, watching him bob over the waves like a seagull. "He looks so happy."

"Oh, he is," she says, still smiling. "He loves the water... Actually, he used to stay at the Anderson Cottage on the first floor, back in the day."

"Really?" I say, feeling the heat rise to my cheeks at the thought of Desmond.

"Yes. His story is pretty special," she says, fidgeting with her diamond. "Back in the fifties, when he was living on the first floor of the Anderson Cottage, he met a girl who ended up being the love of his life, but her father wouldn't allow them to be together."

"Wow," I say, absorbing this information as I observe him from shore. "That's so sad."

"It is," Maggie agrees. "They both got married and went on with their lives, but the truth is, Art never forgot about Katie. And just this past summer, Katie came to live at WVC, and you wouldn't believe it... They got married!"

"That's, wow, that's just incredible."

"Yes, such an amazing story. That was the same summer.... That was the summer West and I finally got together too," she explains, trying to hide her lovestruck smile but coming up short.

"When is your wedding?" I ask, holding my gaze on her ring.

"It's coming up!" she squeals. "I actually have a meeting

with our wedding planner today..." Her eyes grow wide as she waves frantically over my shoulder. "Wendy!" she shouts. "Wendy, your visitors are here!"

I cast an aside glance to my right and notice an elderly woman slowly shuffling toward us with a cane. Her silver hair glistens underneath the sunlight, and her smile is so wide it seems to encompass her entire face. On her shoulder, she carries a large reusable Target bag so red that it matches her cherry-red lipstick. "Beckett!" she calls out, half laughing and half crying. "Oh, Beckett, how I have missed you."

* * *

BREAKFAST WITH WENDY is a huge success. She is thrilled to hear that we are staying at the Anderson Cottage and that Bex is interested in learning more about his birth parents. She asks me if I have had a chance to go through the boxes that were delivered from storage. I am honest, explaining that things have been so busy for us that aside from a few photos, no, I have not been able to go through them yet.

"I'm sure this hasn't been easy," she acknowledges. "We really are truly grateful for your help, Tessa."

"Of course," I say as we wrap up our breakfast on the beach. "Do you happen to know *why* Samantha and David chose me? I mean, don't get me wrong... I wouldn't trade this for anything," I say, motioning to Bex, who is once again playing on his phone. "It's just that... I didn't know the family well."

Wendy nods and places a comforting hand on my shoulder. "I know enough," she whispers. "To know that she made the right choice. Just seeing you with Beckett, you are what he needs. I think that's the most important, don't you?"

"Of course," I agree, allowing her compliment to wash over me, completely aware that her approval validates my many insecurities over the issue. "And I'm sorry... I don't mean to sound insensitive. You must miss your granddaughter so much."

"I do. But I keep her here," she says, motioning to her heart. "Just like I keep all of the loved ones that are now lost." She reaches down onto the floor and scoops up her Target bag. "I want you to take this," she instructs. "And when you have some time to yourself.... Well, you will see..."

One might think that after being left at a cliffhanger like that, I would run home, tear open the bag, and rip through it until I find some sort of sign about why Sam left Bex with me. But I can't because we don't have time. Our breakfast goes forty-five minutes longer than I anticipated, which leaves me only twenty minutes to get Bex ready for his first swim lesson with Desmond.

"Go get changed," I tell Bex as we run up the stairs to the third floor. My fingers slide along the gray siding all the way to the top. "Don't forget your swim shirt."

"Okay, Mom."

"Get the sunblock out when you're done," I call. I run down the hall into my bedroom and rip off my black leggings and brightly colored blouse. I shimmy into my favorite red bikini, pull my coverup from the dirty clothes pile, and toss my hair into a messy bun. A knock on the porch door startles me, and as I check my Apple Watch, which reads 12:00 sharp, that Desmond is here to pick up Bex.

"Just a sec!" I call from down the hallway. I grab my morning coffee cup from the counter and dump it in the sink with the other dirty dishes, all the while cursing my time management skills. "Bex, are you ready?" I call down the hall.

"Almost!"

I fling open the storm door, harder than I intend to, to find Desmond on the other side. For whatever reason, he appears even more attractive than he was at the surf shop, and I can't tell if I'm turned on or annoyed by this. "What's up," he says, one arm leaning against the side of the house and the other on his hip. He wears the same orange swim shorts that he wore yesterday, only this time he seems to have forgotten a shirt.

"What's up," I repeat, placing my own hand on my hip. I bite down on my lower lip and silently scream at myself to stop drooling over my son's swim instructor. But in my defense, his muscles are the definition of washboard abs, and they do that thing that lower side abs can do that I've only actually seen on television, and I'm just *not* okay. "He's almost ready," I say, my words jumbling together and forming more of one entire word, not a complete sentence. "Breakfast ran late."

"Cool," he says, still smiling at me.

"Cool."

"I'm ready, Mom," Bex says, appearing next to me. He studies Desmond's beach attire and then looks down at his long-sleeve compression shirt.

"Do you have your water shoes?" I ask, beginning to search the porch for them.

"I don't want them," he says firmly.

"Really?"

"Really," he says. "And I don't think I want the shirt either."

WE FOLLOW Desmond across the street onto Long Sands Beach, where he instructs me to drop my beach chair and set up camp by the lifeguard stand. I barely have enough time to put sunblock on Bex before he darts off to his lesson. I don't know whether to be proud of him for facing his fear of the ocean, or to panic. Because Bex can be brave when he wants to be, but once he starts to freak out, sometimes there's no calming him down.

For this reason, I inch my beach chair closer to the shore. This way, I can hear what Desmond is saying to Bex, and of course, I can be there if he needs me. Desmond is facing the calm waters of low tide, his hands on his hips as Bex does the same. I realize now that I've never seen my son so relaxed, especially in this kind of situation. What is it about this guy that intrigues him so much? I can't hear them, which frustrates me, but after a few moments of trying, I give up and decide to take some time to myself. My gut tells me, though, that I'm going to want a picture of this moment, and I can't resist. I use my cell phone to take a picture of Des and Bex standing side by side, looking at the horizon.

Tessa: How cute is this? *(Insert Photo)*

Kayla: OMG, adorable. Do you think he will go in?

Tessa: We will see. I've been banned to the beach chair.

Desmond begins kicking through the shallow surf and talking in the animated way that he does, his entire body telling a story of some sort. He turns toward me, acknowledges my presence with a nod, and continues talking to Bex, and I can't resist. I snap another photo, this time capturing the entire essence of Desmond the Surf Guy.

Tessa: This is what I'm up against. *(Insert Photo)*

Kayla: HOLY ABS

Tessa: No kidding. I quit life.

Kayla: Why? This could be GOOD! Ask him to go for a drink. DO IT.

Tessa: He probably isn't even old enough to drink. Way too young for me.

Kayla: Tess, you're 29…NOT 80.

. . .

I LOOK up from my phone just in time to see Desmond and Bex kicking their feet through the icy Atlantic. Desmond continues into the surf until the water is up to his shins while Bex hesitates. "Oh, no," I whisper. "You've got this, Little Monkey."

Bex shakes his head from side to side, turns away from Desmond, and begins storming out of the water. Desmond follows closely behind, and within seconds they are both standing in front of my chair, a larger-than-life frown spread across my son's face.

"How's it going?" I ask innocently.

"He's a champ," Des says, high-fiving Bex.

"Okay," I say, a bit confused. "So... we got up to our ankles today?"

"We aren't even close to done," he explains. "He wants you to come in with us."

"Me?"

"Is that a problem?" Desmond asks, looking me up and down.

"No," I say, my tone a bit more defensive than I intend. "But you said—"

"I know what I said," he interrupts. "But I reevaluated. And I think you should be there."

"Okay," I say, pulling myself from my beach chair. I peel my coverup over my head and toss it aside. "Let's do it."

Desmond pauses for a beat, and I can feel the heat of his stare on my body. "Let's do it."

I follow him and Bex back to where the water meets the sand. For a moment, I am terrified. I so badly want Bex to swim, but in the same breath I feel like I am putting way too much pressure on him. Bex has valid reasons for not wanting to swim in the ocean. He has a *diagnosis*. But if he is willing to follow Desmond out into the frigid Maine waters in late June, so am I. "It's cold," I say as the water tickles my toes.

Des turns around and gives me a warning with his eyes.

"But it's great!" I say, sounding overly cheerful.

"It's beautiful," Desmond agrees. "I was telling Bex that he always needs to face the ocean head-on. I explained to him that we never turn our backs to the ocean."

"Good advice," I say, kicking through the surf. I watch Bex, and I'm completely amazed that he has made it up to his shins before freezing like a statue.

"I can't do it," Bex calls. "Mom, I want to go back!"

"Okay, buddy—" I start.

"You've got this, little dude," Desmond reassures.

"I can't," Bex repeats, his bottom lip beginning to quiver. "The sand and the rocks… they are hurting my feet… and it's so cold."

"It's okay, Bex. We can—"

"We're not going back. Not yet," Desmond says firmly, his eyes narrowing and meeting my gaze. "You can do this," he says seriously and with more authority than I have heard in his tone thus far. "Do you trust me, Bex?"

Bex looks from Desmond to me then back at Desmond. "Yes," he says in his quietest voice, his bottom lip quivering.

"Do *you* trust me?" he asks me, the volume of his voice growing louder by the second.

"I… I barely know you," I confess. I look from Desmond to Bex and back again. "I need to take care of him," I say, turning away from him and approaching my son.

"This isn't going to work," he says, his tone serious and his words short.

"I'm sorry," I say, looking back toward him. "Maybe… maybe this wasn't a good idea?"

"But I want to swim, Mom," Bex yells, clearly frustrated.

I shake my head and throw my hands in the air. "I can't fix this!" I cry. "I don't know how I can help either of you." I wipe a tear from underneath my sunglasses, hoping that neither of them has spotted it.

"TJ," Desmond says, softly this time. "I need you to trust me."

"It's just…" My stare freezes on Bex, my son.

"It's just what?" Desmond challenges, the waves' sounds growing louder and louder and making it harder for me to process my own feelings. "You either trust me or you don't."

My knees begin to tremble, and my stomach flips. I shake my head and close my eyes, and when I open them, Desmond's face is inches from mine. I leap back, startled, and begin to turn away. He places a reassuring hand on my shoulder, and when he does, the energy from his fingertips crackles through my body like electricity. He places his hands on either side of my face. "Look at me," he says, calmly. I look at Bex out of the corner of my eye and am suddenly embarrassed by this moment of weakness. "Look at *me*." Desmond gently lifts my sunglasses off my eyes and up onto my head. His stare is locked on mine, and for a moment I can see into his soul. I want to look away, but I force myself to stare into his amazingly blue eyes. Then I can't breathe. "Do you trust me?"

"Yes," I whisper. "I do."

"That's a start."

"But I still don't know how to help him."

"He says you don't believe that he can do it."

"What?" I gasp. "That's not true."

Desmond releases my shoulders from his hands and places his hands on his hips. "Tell him," he insists. "Tell him he can do it."

I bolt towards Bex and pull him close to me in a big bear hug, the waves crashing over my shins and his knees. "You can do this," I say in my strongest mom voice ever.

"Tell him again," Desmond instructs.

"Bex, I know you can do this. It's going to be uncomfortable for a minute, but you are strong. You can do it."

"I don't think I can," he says, a small tear trickling down the side of his face. I want to scoop him up and run away with him. Putting him in this situation is torture. "I want to, but I don't think I can."

"You want to boogie board with Zoe, right?"

"Yes."

"Then you need to learn how to swim in the ocean. It's just like the pools you swim at when we stay at hotels with Grandma and Grandpa… It's just a little bigger and a little rougher. You can do this, Bex. I believe in you."

Desmond reaches his hand out to Bex. The two of them walk farther into the ocean, hand in hand. Bex makes it up to his waist before crying out and giving up. He bolts from the water and retreats up the sandy hill and back to my chair. I watch as he digs through my beach bag and finds his towel.

"I hate this," I confess to Desmond, covering my face with my hands. I groan, frustrated for my son, since I don't think I've ever wanted anything this badly for him in his entire life.

"Don't hate this," he says with a chuckle. "He's doing great."

"He is?"

"He is. So why aren't you?"

"It's just… I… There is a lot you don't know…" I look anywhere but at Des.

"There's a lot I don't know?"

I put my hands on my hips and stare at the waves as they break on my legs. "It's complicated."

"Complicated how?"

"It's just a long story, Desmond," I say, finally looking up and making eye contact with him once again.

"I have time… for your long story."

I study him, wondering if he is serious or feeling bad for us. "You do?"

"Hells yeah... How about tonight? Over drinks? I do live right downstairs from you."

Blood rushes to my cheeks, and I know he can sense my embarrassment. "Are you asking me on a date?"

"I'm asking you to have a drink with me."

"I don't date," I reaffirm.

"I got you," he says, chuckling. "It's just a drink. So you can tell me about your son and this unusually complicated situation."

"Are you even old enough to drink?" I blurt.

"Yes, actually." If he's offended, he doesn't let on.

"I'm going to be thirty in September," I say, hating myself for oversharing, but relief floods over me once I do.

"I'm twenty-three," he says. "Anything else you need to know about me before agreeing to a drink? Shoe size? Social Security number? Emergency contact?"

"Blood type?" I joke.

"A positive."

"I was kidding."

"I know."

"Let me think about it, okay?"

"Sure. But I'll be downstairs at 7:00. You can let me know what you like to drink, or you can just let me surprise you."

"Surprise me," I say, suddenly impressed with his determination and surprised by my boldness. "It might be closer to 8:00. I'll want to make sure Bex is settled."

* * *

At 8:00 sharp, I check on Bex for the third time and begin making my way down the Anderson Cottage's outside stairs. After three outfit changes and multiple texts to Kayla asking what a person wears for "just drinks" at a beach cottage, to which she responds that a six-year age difference is not too much of a gap, I finally settle on my favorite jeans, my most comfortable pink camo tank top, and a gray zip-up hoodie. Now, as I skip down the steps to the first floor, I hear conversation from the second floor and wonder if this is a good time to introduce myself to Sean and Cassidy. I decide to wait, though. Instead, I continue down the stairs to the cottage's first floor and knock twice on the storm door. When nobody answers, I attempt to knock again, but someone flings the door open. Des is standing there with that smile of his glued to his face.

"Hi," he says, his gaze locked on mine.

"Hi," I say, frozen like a statue.

"Are you coming in, or what?"

"Yeah," I say. "But this isn't a date."

"Right."

Desmond holds the door for me as I enter the cottage. It is smaller than the third floor, I notice. Upon entering, I see a tiny kitchen to my right and a living room straight ahead. A quaint brick fireplace gives off a welcoming vibe with a love seat and a single reclining chair. "So, this is the famous first floor," I say, hoping Des gets my Nubble Light book reference.

"Indeed," he replies. "According to Sean Anderson, this is where the magic happened with Gwendoline and Joey."

"So long ago," I say, reflecting on how much has happened in this home over the years.

"You read the books?" he asks.

"I've read the first two," I admit. "I still have to read the third. I don't get a lot of down time."

"I've read all three," he says, opening the fridge and poking his head inside.

"You read?"

"Yeah. Does that surprise you?"

"No, not at all," I say awkwardly, but somehow it does.

"I ordered takeout," he explains. "It should be here soon."

"Thanks. I didn't eat yet... so thank you."

"I went with wine."

"Wine?"

"White wine. You strike me as a sauvignon blanc kind of girl."

"That's... that's amazing," I say, because I am in fact a sauvignon blanc kind of girl.

"It's actually my favorite," he admits. "It's what I had in the fridge."

I study him for a beat, thankful that he has chosen to put clothes on, even if they're only athletic pants and a white T-shirt. It is easier to hold a conversation when my mind isn't wandering in all the wrong places. "That works, then," I say. "I'll have a glass of wine."

* * *

ONE GLASS of wine turns to three, and before I know it, we have devoured an entire calzone together. I have told him the story of Bex, the plane crash that killed his parents, and the strange guardianship nomination. At first, I don't think Des believes me. But by the time I'm done telling the story, we've polished off the third glass of wine, and I'm crying about Noah, I think he finally does.

"So, you actually saw the ring?"

"Yup," I say, wiping a tear from my eye with the sleeve of my sweatshirt.

"And he didn't propose?"

"Nope."

"And you haven't dated since... since Noah?" he asks, eyes wide.

"No," I affirm. We are seated on the couch, facing the fireplace. My body is turned toward his, and my knee is pressed against his shin. The feeling of his leg against mine soothes me in a way I can't quite explain, and I wonder if he feels it too. "But we can't say the same for you," I say, surprised by my boldness.

"What do you mean?"

"I've seen the ladies coming and going from the first floor," I say. "You have a *lot* of girlfriends."

"I don't have a lot of girlfriends," he says, laughing in between his words.

I hold my empty wine glass toward him and gesture for more wine. He stands and enters the kitchen. Soon he returns with the bottle and refills my glass. "I counted three," I say, satisfied with myself. "Skinny redhead in short shorts, tiny blonde with fancy car, and tall girl, very athletic looking."

"They aren't girlfriends."

"Oh," I say, nodding. "Friends with benefits."

"No," he says, clearly amused. "I'm just talking to them."

"I'm sorry, what?"

"Talking."

"You lost me."

"It's like dating… It's non-exclusive… like, I'm getting to know them."

"Oh," I say, still confused. "I think that's the same as dating."

"Maybe," he agrees. "But nothing serious." He pauses for a beat to wipe a strand of hair out of my eye. My gaze locks on his, and for a moment, my breath is caught somewhere between my lungs and my throat.

"But this isn't a date," I remind him, wondering for a minute why this is such an important detail. *Why don't I date?* I ask myself. I'm sure it's the wine that is allowing me to put my guard down. But the part of me that has been through Hell and back is not letting me off the hook so easily.

"I got you," he says. "Not a date."

"And no talking," I say, slurring my words a bit.

"Well, I mean, technically we are talking. There is no way around that."

"You know what I mean."

"I know."

"Bex," I say. "He's the most important." I sip my wine and place my glass on the coffee table next to me. I turn my body towards Des and pull my knees close to my chest. "I made the decision to put him first."

"You are crushing it."

"I am?"

"Hells, yeah."

"Thanks," I say, breathing a sigh of relief. "I gave up a lot for him. I just want to do a good job." My eyes start to become heavy. I curse myself for drinking too much.

"Do you still talk to Noah?" Des asks, eyes wide.

"Nope. Just saw him on Insta," I admit. "He's dating Barbie." I rest my chin in my hand, but my arm gives in, and I fall forward and collapse onto his torso. I've lost control of my ability to make good choices, and I begin to trace my fingers over his stomach. "Holy abs," I blurt. I look up at him in horror as his eyebrows rise in amusement. "Shit! Did I just say that out loud?"

"You did," he says, chuckling. "And I think we need to get you home."

"Good idea," I say. "If you can just forget this entire conversation, that would be excellent."

"Oh, I don't think I'm forgetting this anytime soon," he gloats. Desmond helps me to my feet and walks me up three flights of stairs to the third floor of the Anderson Cottage. "You should drink water," he says. "It will help."

"Hangovers suck," I agree. "It's why I don't drink."

"Goodnight, TJ," he says, holding onto my shoulders and pulling me into a quick embrace. His skin feels warm against mine, and he smells good. Like fresh salt air, cologne, and wine.

I pull back from his hug and trace my fingers along the side of his face, grinning at him through my drunken haze. "Goodnight, Desmond... Des... Desmond. Thank you... for everything. You're like... you're like a freaking angel or something."

"I'm no angel," he says, tucking a strand of my brunette tresses behind my ear. "Trust me."

"I don't know about that," I say, backing up and entering the cottage. "You might just be ours."

IN THE PRESENT

TESSA

June 2022

A week has passed since our first swim lesson with Desmond. Little by little, Bex has grown more and more comfortable in the water. Earlier this week, when he was melting down over the water being cold and the sand hurting his feet, Des let him run out and run back in as many times as he needed. "Sometimes you need to go backward a bit in order to move forward," he explained. After about an hour of running in and out of the frigid surf with Desmond, Bex grew comfortable enough to stay in for his lesson... so much so that Desmond got Bex to dunk under the water. I had captured it on my phone... Bex going under and Desmond lifting him up and holding him over his head like an athlete showing off a trophy. Now I have posted that image and a selfie to my Instagram Story... Desmond, Bex, and me chest deep in the ocean, celebrating Bex's victory. I rewatch the video repeatedly, sometimes zooming in on Bex and the look of shock on his face after coming up out of the water, roaring like he just scored the winning touchdown of the Super Bowl. Other times, I focus on Des, welcoming the opportunity to check him out in private, or even just to admire his and Bex's exhilarated expressions as they celebrate their success.

I dig my toes in the sand and watch in anticipation as Bex heads out into the waves with Zoe and his new friend Ellie. He was going to wait until the Fourth of July celebration to try out his boogie board, but his sudden interest in Ellie has lit a fire under him, and he is unstoppable.

"He's like a new kid!" Kayla exclaims as she watches her nephew in the water.

"I can't even…" I say.

"It must be hard to process," Kayla finishes for me.

"It's not even that… I'm just so grateful," I say, obviously referring to Desmond. "I guess I'm just… speechless." I pause for a beat, considering our chemistry. We've exchanged some obvious flirting over the past few days—innocent comments about spending more time together and jabs at Noah for letting me get away. Other moments were a bit more difficult to sort out. A casual hand on my shoulder while he talked to me about Bex and his progress, Desmond's body brushing against mine in situations where there was plenty of room for both of us to have our own space. There is no denying that we share a connection of some sort.

"Dear Lord, are you smiling? Tessa… is that a smile on your face?" Kayla's voice cracks through my daydream, and I freeze, realizing that she's right. I've been smiling without even realizing it.

"I guess I am," I say, trying to play it cool.

"I need to know," she says, like a middle school girl trying to get the dirt on her friend's new crush. "Is this a Bex smile or a Des smile?"

"It's—" I start, but I stop as Kayla's friend Hazel rejoins our circle of beach chairs. Hazel dated my brother, Lucas, through most of high school. I was only in seventh grade at the time, and I wanted to be *just* like her. They broke up the day before their high school graduation, and I remember it like it was yesterday. Lucas had given Hazel an ultimatum about her going away to college in Florida, since long-distance relationships were not really his jam. Hazel, of course, being the strong-willed woman she was, chose Florida over Lucas. My brother didn't cry often, but when he returned home from talking with Hazel that day, he was so devastated that I thought someone had died.

"They look good out there!" Hazel says as she plops down next to me. "Once I sit, I might not get up," she says, pointing at her belly.

"How far along are you?" I ask.

"Just about seven months," Hazel replies, hands on her belly.

"Do you know what you're having?" I ask.

"Warren and I are having a boy," Hazel says, her smile beaming from ear to ear.

"That's so exciting," I say. "Congratulations. Boys are the best."

"Do you have a name picked out?" I ask.

"We do, actually. He's going to be a Junior."

"That's the sweetest," I say. I study her belly and shake away some negative feelings that wash over me. Noah and I were going to start a family. I had always been a huge fan of family names and wanted so badly to name a child after Noah, just as he was named after his father. That obviously didn't happen, and on top of that, I never got to experience pregnancy or childbirth, and a part of me wonders if I ever will.

As if reading my mind and trying to change the subject, Kayla chimes in, "Big date tonight?"

"It's not a date."

"Um... yes, it is," Kayla argues. She turns toward Hazel and points an accusing finger in my direction. "Tessa seems to think that a dinner out with a totally *hot* guy isn't a date."

"He's my son's swim instructor," I clarify. "And I don't date... We are just... talking."

"Oh gosh," Hazel chimes in. "That's what Ellie and her friends say. They aren't dating, they are talking."

"It's a thing," I insist.

"No," Hazel corrects. "When it's a *thing*, it's official."

"I can't keep up," Kayla whines. "All I know, Tessa, is you better be ready for tonight. Because I'm telling you right now... this boy likes you, and I can tell that you like him too."

"I don't date," I reaffirm.

"Why not?" Hazel asks, sounding genuinely concerned.

I close my eyes and inhale deeply. "I have my son to think about. I just, I don't want to be distracted." I open my eyes and stretch my arms overhead. "It's just easier to not date."

Hazel thinks for a moment. "I felt that way once," she said, rubbing her belly with one hand and drinking her water with the other. "I was a single mother, living in Florida, trying to raise my daughter. Dating didn't even seem like a possibility—"

"Then her daughter was kidnapped," Kayla interjects.

"I remember reading about that in Sean's book," I confess.

"I had completely sworn off trusting anyone. But I got some great advice from an old friend..."

"What was it?" I ask, hopeful for her to tell me something either truly inspirational or affirm that dating Des is not a good idea.

She thinks for a moment and smiles. "Love without hesitation," she says. "The only thing worse than getting your heart broken is living with the regret that comes with not letting go."

"Damn," I say, rolling my eyes. "That's good."

"Now you need to go on that date," Kayla says.

"Yup," I agree. "Now I have no choice."

* * *

I DROP Bex off at Kayla's for a sleepover and race home to get ready in time. I jump in the shower, get dressed, and do my hair and makeup in under forty-five minutes. *I can't believe I'm going on a date*, I think. I haven't let myself get to this point in years, but it feels like it's time. Besides, I trust Desmond in a way I've never really trusted anyone... maybe even Noah, which blows my mind, considering Desmond and I haven't known each other that long at all. But even still, I wasn't surprised when he asked me out. My mind keeps skipping back to our past few encounters that were textbook flirting and then of course the occasional hand on my shoulder or back while we talked. We had been standing side by side, watching Bex trudge through the bigger-than-usual waves, when Desmond asked me out. We were frozen like statues watching him, our arms touching, the heat from his body warming my chilled arms but also my tired soul.

"I want to take you to dinner," he had said, gaze locked on the horizon.

"I think I'd like you to take me to dinner," I had replied, my stare set on Bex as he began falling backward into oncoming waves. "But this is so not a date."

That was earlier in the week. Now, I check my Apple Watch, which reads 6:45 pm. Desmond will be picking me up any minute. I study my reflection in the mirror, and I am overly thankful that Kayla has let me borrow an outfit for the evening, a short floral-print tie-front cutout cocktail dress. According to Kayla, it's the perfect compromise between showing off some cleavage with a little tummy while still leaving *something* to the imagination. I gather my hair over my shoulders and check my makeup one last time, butterflies taking over my insides like they are eating me alive.

Des knocks on the door at 7:00 sharp. I answer the door, and he stands there in that way that he does, just smiling at me like he is up to no good. He wears jeans and a button-down top. The blue in his shirt makes his eyes pop even brighter than usual, if that is at all possible. "I would have brought you flowers," he says, his smile unwavering. "But you gave me specific instructions that this was not a date… although… that dress says otherwise," he says, pulling me close to him and wrapping his arm around my lower back. I lean into him, and for a moment, I consider confessing that this is one hundred percent a date, but instead I pull back and give him the most flirtatious smile I can muster up. Winking, I say, "You should always bring flowers."

DESMOND TAKES me to dinner at the York Harbor Inn. We sit by a window overlooking the ocean. We make small talk at first, but after a couple of glasses of wine, I become an open book once again. Desmond asks me about Bex's family and why they chose me for custody of their son. I tell him that I don't have all the answers, but I mention the books that Wendy gave me at the retirement home last week. "You haven't read them yet?" he asks between bites of his steak.

"No," I admit. "There is a part of me that wants to know, but there is another part of me that doesn't. Bex… he's my son… that's the most important thing, right?"

This is the last serious thing we talk about, because somewhere between dessert and asking for the check, he holds my hand... not the kind of hand-holding reserved for cute, lighthearted moments in Hallmark movies but the kind of hand-holding that consists of Des running his fingernails softly over my forearm while making eyes at me. I'm pretty sure this is considered foreplay, and I can't get out of the restaurant fast enough.

The ride from the York Harbor Inn to the Anderson Cottage is less than ten minutes. That, thanks to a shared bottle of wine, is the amount of time it takes me to convince myself that I am indeed ready to date again and ready for anything this night might throw at me. *Let it go, Tessa,* I tell myself as Desmond takes my hand and leads me into the first floor of the Anderson Cottage. I am determined to let go of Noah and the heartache of the past six years.

"Are you good?" Desmond asks as he unlocks the door and pulls me inside. His hands are already wrapped around my waist as he leans me up against the wall between the door and the kitchen counter.

"Oh, I'm good," I reassure him, running my fingers through his thick, dark hair.

He squints his eyes and narrows his gaze, looking at me in a way he hasn't before... almost like we are sharing a juicy secret, or he is undressing me with his eyes. I can't really tell which. He pulls me closer to him once again and presses his lips to my cheek, the closest we have come to sharing a kiss. I close my eyes and drop my head back, allowing it to rest against the wall, meanwhile tugging his face closer to me. "Yes," I say, my words coming out somewhere between a whisper and a cry.

His lips move over my chin and up to my ear as he presses my body against the wall, curling his arms under me and pressing me tighter against him. His hands explore my body freely, and when I open my eyes and my gaze meets his,

I melt even more than I thought possible. I trace the sides of his face with my fingers and pull his face close to mine. My lips blend with his in a long and passionate kiss, and I allow his hands to trace my lower back, my thighs, and under my dress. With every touch and movement, my knees grow weaker, and my body becomes more alive. "Des," I say, unable to get close enough to him. I untuck his shirt and trace the outline of his torso with my fingers, beginning to unbutton his shirt as fast as I can. "Holy abs," I joke.

"TJ, you sure you're good with this?" he asks, his tone serious. "We can slow down. It's okay."

"I'm good, really… I just… I need this—you, Des… I need you. Please don't stop kissing me."

"I need you too," he confesses as he lifts me up in one easy sweep. He wraps my legs around his torso and carries me down the hall to the bedroom. I can't remove my dress fast enough, and before I know it, Desmond and I are fully undressed, and I am lying on my back in his bed with him on top of me. In less than a breath, we are moving together in unison, and I'm overwhelmed with the intensity of our connection, both physically and emotionally.

"Des," I cry out repeatedly, while he touches me in all the right places and whispers all the right things. I draw my head back and allow this person, this man, to help me feel things I have secretly wanted for so long but didn't think I deserved. His hands on my hips, his face in my neck, my hands in his hair. I study him intently, taking everything in and allowing myself to surrender to the feelings and emotions that have taken control of my body.

"You're amazing," he whispers as I pull him as close to me as humanly possible, wishing that this moment could last forever. I trace my fingers along his arms, over his tattoos, onto his shoulders and his back and hold him as tight as I can, determined to glue the memory of the two of us together in my mind, for as long as I live.

When it is over, I keep my hold on him. I fall asleep in his arms, my face nuzzled in the place where his neck meets his chest, and I worry about nothing… except for what I need to do to ensure that I can experience this man, in this way, again.

IN THE PRESENT

TESSA

June 2022

Two days have gone by since the date, and I can't get Des out of my mind. I try with all my entire being to carry on with business as usual, but it is nearly impossible. I focus most of my energy on the Fourth of July party we are having at the Anderson Cottage in just a few short days. But even with the party planning and the grocery shopping, I have only one thing on my mind—Desmond Spencer.

Hanging on the beach with Lucas, Kayla, and their friends has been the hardest. I can see their mouths moving, and I know they are talking to me, but my vision is clouded by images of a completely naked Desmond hovering over me. I hear all the words he whispered in my ear (some appropriate, some not) more clearly than the words that people are saying to me. I can still feel the warmth of his body against me. I have locked away his sweet smell in my mind.

Now, as I sip my coffee on the third-floor porch of the Anderson Cottage, I close my eyes and allow the sunlight to wash over me, and for the first time in a long while, I wonder if I'm happy. It was something I hadn't even considered a possibility for so many reasons. But now... Desmond. Things are just different now, because of him.

We haven't gotten any alone time since our date, and I've been counting down the seconds until we can be together again. Last night was a quiet one for Bex and me, since he was recovering from his sleepover, and today we kept things professional when Desmond came to pick him up for his lesson. Both Des and my son appeared shocked when I informed them that I wouldn't be joining them for their lesson today, that I had stuff to do around the cottage.

Bex had skipped down the stairs ahead of us, eager to get things underway, leaving us on the porch alone. Desmond had leaned in for a kiss, and although I was sure he meant it to be quick, I pulled his face down close to mine for a longer one. "I can't get enough of you," he had whispered.

"I know."

"When can I see you again? Tonight?"

"Tonight," I had said between breaths. "Let me see if Kayla wants to take Bex again."

When I asked him if he wanted to sleep over with Zoe again, his eyes grew wide. According to Kayla, Bex and Ellie had grown quite fond of each other, and they were already trying to find ways to hang out without making things too obvious. Kayla arranged to take Zoe, Ellie, and Bex for pizza on Short Sands Beach and promised to keep an eye on them. The thought of him liking a girl had been a shock to my system, to say the least. I hadn't seen it coming. Part of me was over-the-moon excited for him, while the mama-bear part of me struggled a tiny bit.

I open the porch door to the cottage, coffee cup in hand,

and prepare for the one thing I promised myself I would do—read the books given to me by Wendy Jones, Bex's great grandmother. As much as I don't want to know the entire story, I need to know the truth... for Bex.

I retrieve the Target shopping bag from the floor of my bedroom and empty the contents onto my bed. The books appear to be journals, since their covers are marked with dates and Sam's maiden name. I trace my fingers over the inscriptions made in black Sharpie marker and allow the reality of this situation to hit me. These journals date back to before Sam and David were even married. Why on Earth, I wonder, would I need this much information? Could it be like I had assumed? That maybe the connection that Sam and I shared over the Nubble Lighthouse was enough for her to consider me? *You won't know until you read the journal*, I silently scold myself. There are three journals, all with different floral patterns, all labeled Samantha Marie Proctor. They range in time frame from the year 2008 all the way to 2016. "Organized much?" I say out loud, dropping to my pillow with the first journal. "Here we go, Samantha," I whisper to the empty room. "Let's see exactly what you have up your sleeve."

I begin reading quickly, skimming over the perfectly formed cursive writing in search of anything that had to do with me, Maine, or anything relevant. But by the time I get through 2008, I am intrigued by how fast Sam fell for her husband, David. Apparently, they were high school sweethearts (crowned king and queen at the junior prom). I also find it interesting that David was one year ahead of Samantha in high school. Still no mention of either of them spending much time in Maine, which explains why Lucas wouldn't have much recollection of either of them, but she does mention her private high school periodically.

I learn a lot about Samantha. She was a people pleaser

TEN PERCENT OF MY HEART

who worked very hard to make sure those around her were taken care of. Most thoughts, feelings, and concerns expressed in her writing are about others. She missed her mother dearly, who had passed away unexpectedly. Most of her sad entries are about missing her mother and resenting her father for leaving. It seems, based on what she has reflected on in her diary, that Wendy Jones was her caregiver during these times. "If it wasn't for Grandma," Sam wrote, "I never would have made it through this year."

I glance at my watch and realize that I have just about thirty minutes until Desmond and Bex return. As much as I've loved getting to know Sam, I would really like to continue with my day. I begin to skim over the passages until December of 2009, when the tone of Samantha's diary entries transitions suddenly from passionate and true, especially concerning her feelings about David, to harsh and judgmental. I can't quite put my finger on whom, exactly, she was angry with, but she was most definitely not happy. I flip ahead a bit and realize that she didn't seem to get any better as the months went on. By July of 2010, she came across as completely miserable. I do the math based on Bex's birthday, September 22, 2010, and I grow curious... If David and Sam were so in love and serious about their relationship, why would Sam be so down on herself about getting pregnant? Of course, it always sucks when people get pregnant when they aren't ready, especially when they haven't even graduated high school yet. But the horrible things that she is saying about the decisions that she made... they just aren't adding up. And then I read the diary entry that stops me cold. Because it appears that Samantha Allen has fallen in love with more than one person—and the questions that fly through my mind at a million miles per hour become very unsettling, to say the least. "What are you hiding, Sam?" I ask my empty bedroom. And for a moment, the pit that has formed in the bottom of my stomach begins to take over my entire being. I'm not sure why... but I feel like this might change *everything*.

August 20, 2010

    Dear Diary,

    It hadn't been my intention to fall in love. Why would anyone willfully go out of their way to overcomplicate an already picture-perfect life? I am already in love, fully committed to another person. Of course, relationships take work... and although mine has its challenges, we are in a solid place. We are happy... or at least I like to believe that we are.

    I've learned that having feelings for a person, whether that be love, lust, or simply increased dopamine and norepinephrine levels in our brains... is still real. It doesn't play fair, and it surely doesn't play nice. You see, love doesn't take turns. It isn't like the methodical and systematic line for the ladies' room, women filing in one after the other, taking turns as stalls become vacant. And it isn't like moving over in your seat on the bus or the subway, allowing someone else to share space that was comfortably yours. No. When you are already in love and your heart has been fully given to another person, there just isn't enough space for you to fully fall in love with another. It isn't possible, or even fair for that matter, for a person in this predicament to have their cake and eat it too.

    So, if I can't very well dedicate ninety percent of my heart to one person and ten percent to another, where does that leave me? I'll tell you where... determined to shed the ten percent of my soul that has me completely and utterly paralyzed with emotions that were not invited. I need to let them go, and I will move on. I don't have a choice because it's not only about me anymore. There is just too much at stake to give in to this desire. It is time to consider my future... our future.

    I've been told that pain is weakness leaving the body. If that's true, I'm getting stronger by the second. This whole thing, it isn't easy...it's terrifying. We get one shot at this life we live. And this hurt... this loss... these emotions... these tears... they are one hundred percent real. I'll probably be crying those tears forever. Because for the first time in my life, I am backing down from something I want. For the first time in this history of my existence, I am burying a dream.

This ten percent of me... this tiny part that is clinging on for dear life to the distorted possibility of things working out between us could destroy me. So, I'll smile... I'll live... I'll love. And I will fill that tiny void with the joy that comes from watching my child grow, hearing that laugh, experiencing motherhood. No matter how strong a connection I share with that man and what sort of joy he could have brought to my life, it ends now.

Timing can be everything... and in this case, it is my enemy. As these tears trickle down my cheeks like they do day after day, month after month, and probably year after year, I will rest knowing that even though they sting, even though I'll always be a little empty on the inside... I will be whole in other ways... ways I once only imagined. So, to the love that will never be, the love that can never be one hundred percent mine, I will see you in my dreams. Because selfishly, those will always belong to me.

ALWAYS,
    Sam

IN THE PAST

SAMANTHA

December 2009

The ski trip. An innocent getaway to celebrate David's high school graduation. By the time this trip came about, David and I had already been dating for three years, which was why my grandmother finally allowed me to go. She had a soft spot for David, but although she trusted him, she understood young love and was constantly worried about me. At first, she was completely against it. "You are only a junior in high school, Samantha. Don't you think you are a little young for something like this?"

"It's not just the two of us, Grandma," I promised. "We will be with a bunch of other kids."

"Don't do anything stupid," she had warned.

"I won't, I promise."

I knew that she was nervous about David and me "accidentally making a baby," as she often reiterated, but I reminded her that if we were going to accidentally make a baby, we didn't need a ski trip to do it. She had chuckled and pulled me close, kissing me on the forehead and warning me one more time, "No babies."

I had agreed to get out on the mountain with him a few times but was a bit nervous, since my last experience included a bunny slope and a bruised tailbone. "You will be fine," he insisted. "I won't let anything happen to you." Looking back, I wish I had taken some of the advice, any of the advice my grandmother had given me. I sometimes wonder what would have come about if the ski trip never happened in the first place. But I was a teenager, and that kind of freedom was invigorating.

The house was gorgeous, just as David promised. We shared a bedroom on the second floor with a private balcony. My best friend, Jessica, and her boyfriend, Marc, were directly across the hall from us in the other large bedroom. There was a handful of kids on the trip whom I hadn't met yet. Some knew David well, while others (friends of friends) tagged along and landed sleeping-bag space on the third floor, which equaled twelve of us nuzzled away in a snowy New England ski cabin, without a care in the world.

That was, until my first time out on the mountain became a complete catastrophe. I lost control of my skis on my way down the easiest trail and skidded toward a group of ski school students. To avoid knocking them down like bowling pins, I wiped out and flew off the trail and directly into a tree. After four hours at the nearest emergency room with David, I was diagnosed with a concussion and a badly sprained wrist. No more skiing for me.

David had offered to take me home, but I insisted on staying. It was the social aspect of the trip I had been looking forward to the most—that and alone time with my boyfriend, so it didn't seem necessary to leave. Instead, I took full advantage of the most comfortable recliner in the house and decided it would be there, by the wood-burning fireplace, that I would spend my days.

So, there I was, day two of a seven-day ski trip, curled up in my favorite chair, coffee in hand, in my red-and-black flannel pajama pants and David's favorite gray hoodie. Changing into any other clothes seemed pointless, since I didn't have the use of my left hand, and I would be spending the day solo. David did his best to gather my brunette tresses in the best version of a ponytail he could pull off, which was awkward for him because I was taller than him by half an inch. He gave me a lesson in keeping the fire going before taking off for the day on the mountain. I studied the crackling flame as it burned away in the brick fireplace and wondered how long it would be until I grew bored of it, a sudden wave of disappointment washing over me. I sat up and reached for my journal, feeling grateful that I didn't sprain my dominant hand. I sat back in the recliner and began dating the journal entry, determined to make the most out of this day.

"Good morning!" a voice from behind me called out. I tossed my pen down atop my journal and spun my head around as much as I could, my head still pounding a bit. I hadn't realized anyone else was home, but apparently, I was wrong. One of the guys from the third floor brushed past me toward the kitchen, also still in his pajamas. I didn't recognize him from a hole in the wall, but then again, most of my trip had consisted of the emergency room and my bedroom, so it was no surprise that there were friends I hadn't met yet.

"I heard you've had a rough go of it," he called from the kitchen.

"Yes," I agreed, feeling a bit embarrassed. "Skiing is quite lovely until trees get involved." I hold up my bandaged wrist and shrug.

"Yikes," he said, reaching for a coffee mug. "Want a coffee?"

"I had one, thank you."

"I'll be here if you need anything," he said as he added creamer to his coffee.

"You will? Too cool for the slopes?"

He smiled and shook his head. "I don't ski. I just came up for the parties."

"Oh," I said, considering this for a moment. "I tried that approach with my boyfriend, and look where it got me."

"It's kind of badass," he said, taking a sip from his coffee mug.

"Well, I have a concussion too," I brag. "Is that even more badass?"

"No," he said, chuckling. "That's just scary."

I nodded. "It was pretty scary."

My new friend rested his coffee mug on the end table and added a log to the fire. "That's better," he said, admiring the burning flame.

"Thanks for doing that."

"Anytime," he said, taking a seat on the sofa next to me. I studied him for a beat and wondered if this guy planned on invading my space for the entire day, or if he was just going to make small talk with me while he drank his coffee. He was tall and attractive, not so much in an athletic way but just in a cute boy-next-door sort of way. I sipped my coffee from my mug, disappointed that it had already grown cold and too sore to get up from my chair and heat it up. I considered asking him to heat it up for me but instead decided to just keep quiet.

"So, what's your name?" he asked, like an elementary school student on the playground.

"My name?" My mouth curled into a soft smile.

"Yeah."

"Samantha."

"What's your name?" I asked.

"Junior," he said, raising his coffee mug in my direction.

"Junior," I repeated. "It's nice to meet you."

"Tell me about yourself, Samantha," he said, my name rolling off his tongue like a breath of fresh air.

"There isn't much to tell."

"I don't believe that for a second."

* * *

BY DAY five of the ski trip, I had settled into quite the routine. I would wake up, have coffee in my recliner, and spend the day chatting it up with my new friend, Junior. We had one job, to keep the fire going for the day's duration. Junior made lunch (his peanut butter and jelly sandwiches were on point) and we would top it off with hot chocolate. By the time the sun started to go down, we would trade our mugs for bottles of beer and eagerly welcome David, Jessica, and the ski group home for a night of pizza, drinks, and good fun.

By day six of the trip, I started to grow sad that the week was coming to an end. Of course, I was enjoying my time with David. The alone time we had in the evenings was still all I had hoped for and more... but I didn't want the week to end. On day six of the ski trip, Junior and I broke out the beers a lot earlier than normal and began playing our own drinking games hours before the crew arrived home. Junior and I sat on the carpet by the fire, both still wearing our pajamas, beers in hand. "Never have I ever cut class," I say, guzzling down my beer, remembering the one time I cut class with Jessica. I peeked out of the corner of my eye and realized that Junior was not drinking. "You've never skipped school?" I shrieked in horror.

"Nope. My mother would kill me."

"Lame," I said, chuckling, but for a moment, I was envious that he *had* a mother. "My mother," I started but then stopped.

"What about your mother?"

"It's nothing."

"It's not nothing," Junior said, his voice growing softer as he placed a comforting hand on my knee.

"She... she passed away."

"Wow, I'm... I'm so sorry."

"Your turn," I say, eager to change the subject. "Never have I ever..."

Junior studied me for a moment, clearly wondering whether to push for more information. He took a swig from his beer and thought for a beat. "I'm really sorry, Sam. That must be really hard." He paused for a moment and locked his eyes on mine. "Never have I ever crashed into a tree... on skis."

"No fair!" I squealed.

"Nope, you have to drink!" he said, laughing at his own joke.

I took a swig of my beer. "Never have I ever been a complete asshole," I said, motioning in his direction. "Drink!"

"But I'm not an asshole," he said, his face growing serious.

"Just drink," I said, ignoring him. "And put another log on the fire, I think it's going out."

Junior stood up from our game and took a long drink of beer, stumbling a bit. He tossed another log on the fire before heading toward the fridge for more beer. He popped them open and returned to our spot on the floor. "Your turn," he said.

"Ugh," I sighed. "I'm sorry I called you an asshole... It was mean of me," I said, slurring my words a bit. I held on to the edge of the coffee table to steady myself. "How many beers have we had?"

"Who even knows."

"A lot," I say, taking another sip.

"You don't think I'm an asshole, then?" he asked, scooching toward me, allowing our knees to touch.

"No, Junior. I think… I think you are pretty great, actually." I reached up and ran my good hand through his blond hair. "Your hair is soft," I said with a giggle, allowing the giddiness from my beer buzz to take control of me.

Junior collected the ends of my ponytail in his fingers and smiled. "Yours is too."

We both burst out laughing, and I chuckled until my insides couldn't handle it anymore. "You're funny," I said between swigs of beer.

"You're…" Junior said, taking a sip of his beer and then pausing. "You're… you're… you're absolutely amazing."

We sat, knees touching, frozen in time in front of the fire. My eyes locked on Junior's, and for a moment, I couldn't think of any logical reason why we couldn't be together. The heat from his knees against mine radiated throughout my entire being. "I think you're amazing too," I whispered, neither of us realizing that the sun was setting in the distance.

"Samantha," Junior whispered, his lips centimeters from mine. "I'm going to kiss you."

"Okay," I replied, my voice a choked whisper.

Junior leaned closer to me and placed his hands on my shoulders. Our lips were the first to touch, and his kiss took my breath away. He helped me onto my back, kissing the tips of my injured fingers and carefully resting my wrist on the pillow. He climbed over me, and the kissing continued. I wrapped my arm around his lower back and pulled him closer to me, all the while thinking of nothing but him. His hands as they ran over my body. The gentle way he helped me out of my T-shirt and pants. How magnificent he looked as he towered over me in the fire's light.

"Junior?" I asked, tracing my hand over his jaw.

"Yeah?"

"Do you believe... in soulmates? Like... the kind you love."

Junior pulled back for a moment, studying me in the darkness. "I didn't... before now."

"Because," I whispered between breaths, "I think I..." My words caught in my throat. I shook my head and pull him in for another kiss.

"Do you think it's the beer talking?" he asked, his lips forming a serious expression.

"Does it matter?" I asked, surprised by my boldness. I tugged at the sides of his pajama pants with one hand and wrapped my legs around his torso, tugging him down onto me the best I could.

"I guess not," he groaned between breaths. "Because I think I love you." Junior shimmied out of his pajama pants and pulled me on top of him. He wrapped my legs around his waist and held my face in his hands, kissing me the entire time we made love.

When it was over, we lay there together by the fire as I drifted off to sleep. I felt like the luckiest girl alive for being able to connect with someone in this way, but in the back of my mind another voice screamed at me. A voice of guilt and shame roared at me like the ocean in a storm. My thoughts exploded at the sound of car doors closing in the garage. I knew that I needed to open my eyes and get up, and I told myself this, but my body did not cooperate. "Samantha, get up!" Junior said, shaking my shoulders.

"Lie back down," I pleaded.

"David is back," Junior shrieked, urgency screaming from within him.

"I think I love you," I whispered in the darkness. "There... I said it."

"You have to get up!" he pleaded, gathering our clothes in one hand and pulling me up off the ground with his other. I stood up, my long naked legs wobbling by the fire's glow, and allowed Junior to drag me up the stairs and lead me to my bedroom. He tossed my clothes next to me as I flopped down on my bed. He shimmied into his pants and T-shirt. "Here," he said, helping me into my pajama pants and tank top. "Get under the covers."

"Okay," I agreed, sliding under the covers and resting my head against the pillow.

"Are you okay?" he asked, continuing to check over his shoulder.

"I'm *really* okay," I replied.

"Okay. I'm going to tell them you had too much to drink and went to sleep, okay?" Junior leaned down to kiss my forehead, but I grabbed the sides of his face and pressed my lips to his. "Goodnight, Samantha," he said before pulling away.

"Please don't go," I begged. But it was too late. Junior was already gone. I buried my face in my pillow and silently begged the room to stop spinning. Allowing the memory of Junior by the fire to consume me.

"Samantha?" a soft voice called from somewhere in the darkness.

"Jessica?"

"Sam, are you all right?"

"Yes," I affirmed, squinting one eye open and smiling at my friend. "I'm actually quite lovely. Why does everyone keep asking me that?"

IN THE PRESENT

NOAH

July 2022

I can think of a million reasons why social media makes life harder. In this case, it is making things impossible. The destruction of my current relationship and the sleepless nights that come from raging insomnia began the day Tessa Walker viewed my Instagram Story. How the hell does someone as educated and successful as me get sucked down a rabbit hole that begins with their ex and a stupid social media app?

At first, she hadn't posted much. It started with a selfie of her and Bex with a guy I had never seen before. His dark, shaggy hair was wet and slicked back, and his tanned skin glistened in the sunlight. It wasn't his washboard abs that made me angry beyond belief. It was that one of his tattooed arms was around Tessa's waist, and the other around was Bex's shoulder. I was on my lunch break when I first laid eyes on this picture, and it was all I could do to continue about my day without wanting to punch something or somebody.

I'm not an angry person by any means, which was why my sudden change in mood really bothered Nadine. At first, I was just a bit short with some of my responses to her routine questions. Then, after about a week of sleepless nights and more of Tessa's Instagram posts, I became irritable over the smallest things and started relying on drinking to calm me down. Nadine was patient at first, but when I didn't open up to her about what was bothering me, it pushed her away. "I think I need some space," she had said, over text. "Let me know when you feel like actually talking about what's got you down."

The phrase *what's got you down* didn't quite justify what I was going through. But really, do I have anyone to blame but myself? I chose to leave Tessa and Bex. I'm the one who bailed on her... not the other way around. So why am I so furious? Tessa started a hashtag on Instagram... #mapoftheirlives. After only a few posts with this hashtag, it became clear that Tessa was taking her son on a journey in remembrance... and I had to assume it was in memory of his parents, the ones that died in the crash. The first post was a photo of Bex eating a gigantic chocolate ice cream cone, beaming-eyed and smiling. The second was of him in front of the Nubble Lighthouse. I recognized the lighthouse from the summer that Tessa and I spent back in her hometown of York, Maine. The third photo was of Tessa and Bex at the arcade on Short Sands Beach. He is holding up handfuls of arcade tickets beside the same shirtless guy from the ocean photo. The last is a selfie of her and her sister-in law, Kayla, in front of a three-story gray cottage tagged with #andersoncottage.

Part of me wishes that Tessa never came up on social media. The other part has been so drawn to following her that it's become a solid obsession. Over the past couple of weeks, it has blown my mind to think about her being back in Maine and with someone... someone who isn't, well, me. Another part of me feels the shame of bailing on her during such an impossible time, especially when we were at such a major turning point in our relationship. I know enough about how the mind works to understand that this guilt and shame has turned to anger, and I'm angry with Tessa. That doesn't make any sense at all, because if this were a movie, I would be guaranteed to be cast as the bad guy.

"There's just so much I didn't tell you," I whisper out loud to the emptiness of my apartment. Today is my day off, and I can't seem to get it together enough to do anything other than lie here, sprawled out on my couch, eating chips, binge watching episodes of *The Good Doctor*, and stalking my ex on Instagram. I pinch my phone screen to zoom in on her face, and I lock eyes with hers in the photograph, but the image disappears quickly, replaced by my mother's name and picture on Facetime. I roll my eyes and ignore the call, but she calls back, and a piece of me feels bad for ignoring her, so I answer.

"Hi, Mom," I say, staring at myself in the small box of the FaceTime call. *I look like crap*, I think, immediately regretting taking the call.

"You look terrible," my mom shouts, not missing a beat. She holds the phone closer to her face than necessary, allowing me to only see her furrowed brow and red lipstick frown. "I'm worried about you. What's wrong?"

"Nothing's wrong, Ma... It's my day off."

"You don't rest on your days off," she challenges.

I close my eyes and run my fingers over my fresh buzz cut. "I'm tired, that's all," I lie.

"Is it that girlfriend of yours, Naomi?"

"Do you mean Nadine?" I grunt, openly frustrated, since this isn't the first time I've corrected this mistake.

"Yes. The nice young woman from the hospital. Are you still together?"

"Maybe... no... I don't know. Listen, Mom... I'm really looking to get some rest. I haven't been sleeping well."

"You should try melatonin," she instructs. "I've been taking that every night, and I've been sleeping like a baby."

"Thanks, Mom, but you know... I am a doctor."

"I know, dear, but you know that mothers always know best."

I smile at this, and for a moment I relax a bit. "I know, Mom. You're right... Maybe I'll try that tonight." *Or something prescription,* I think.

"I'll let you get some rest, then," she says, blowing a kiss into the phone.

"I love you, Mom," I say, suddenly caught off guard that I am feeling somewhat emotional.

"I love you, too, Junior. You take care of yourself."

"Mom," I say with a sigh. "I'm a grown adult... too old for nicknames. Please just call me Noah."

"Goodbye, Junior, I love you."

IN THE PRESENT

TESSA

July 2022

"Is he coming today?" Kayla asks, taking a swig of beer from her red keg cup and studying the party guests, who are gathered across the street on Long Sands Beach. Our Fourth of July party is in full swing. Although I haven't joined the actual party yet, I've been content hanging out on the deck of the third floor with Kayla. It's been quite some time since I've attended a party of any kind, and aside from a few friends of Kayla and Lucas, I really don't know many people here.

"Who?" I ask, playing dumb. I smile at Kayla, who wears a white crop top that reads Let Freedom Ring in red letters over the American flag.

"You know who," she says, punching me playfully in the arm.

"Desmond will be here around dinnertime," I explain, trying my best to keep a straight face. However, when it comes to Des, my face does this involuntary goofy smiling thing that happens before I realize it. "He had some lessons this afternoon."

"That's good," she says, looking out at the horizon. "I really want to meet him…this guy who makes you so smiley."

"Stop it," I say, half laughing, half annoyed. I pull the fabric of my royal-blue sundress over my knees and press down on my left leg to stop the bouncing. "I keep forgetting that you haven't met him," I say. I shake my head in awe, feeling like I have known Desmond for my entire life. My brain knows this isn't the case, but my heart begs to differ because I can't imagine my life without him… which is scary and completely nuts for many reasons. The first and most obvious reason is that we haven't even known each other for a month. Second, we are in two completely different phases of our lives. I am a twenty-nine-year-old single mother with a full-time career, and he is a twenty-three-year-old surf instructor who rents a beach cottage as his permanent residence.

"Are you guys, like, together? Officially?" Kayla asks, gathering her dark hair over one shoulder.

"Who even knows," I sigh, taking another swig of my beer. "I'm totally lost when it comes to dating in this generation.… I can't remember if we are talking or if we are a thing." I release an exaggerated sigh. "I think I'm just too old-fashioned for this."

"I can't even imagine," Kayla agrees. "Especially the social media piece."

I nod, thinking about my secret obsession with Noah's Instagram account. Even after Des has swept me off my feet, a piece of me can't stop stalking Noah on social. "All right," I say, eager to change the subject. "I'm pretty sure my brother has had enough with watching the kiddos."

"Don't even worry about him," Kayla insists. "Last I checked, he was boogie boarding with Bex and Zoe."

I smile, still in disbelief over my son overcoming his challenges in such a short time. I am completely sucked back into the gratitude I feel for Des and how much he has changed our lives. "Even still," I say, "I wouldn't mind checking on Bex."

* * *

AN HOUR LATER, Kayla and I have settled in our beach chairs on Long Sands amongst other party guests. Hazel sits to my right, balancing a bottle of water on her pregnant belly, and Kayla to my left. Bex, Zoe, and Ellie continue to conquer the waves on their boogie boards.

"Teeej!" Lucas calls from down the beach. "There is someone I want you to meet." Lucas and Warren stroll towards us with a couple I haven't met before. The man, who is tall with short blond hair, wears a white T-shirt and denim shorts. The woman's strawberry-blond hair is pulled back into a French braid, and it takes about two seconds for me to figure out these two must be Sean and Cassidy.

"Cassidy and Sean, this is my sister, TJ," Lucas says, nodding in my direction. Sean extends his hand for a handshake. I rise from my beach chair and shake Sean's hand.

"Sean," he states. "Sean Anderson."

"It's no nice to meet you," I say, getting all sorts of starstruck. "I love your books."

"Thanks," he says, the corners of his mouth turning up into a smile. "I'm glad you enjoyed them."

"Oh, I did," I say more quickly than I mean to. "I haven't read the third one yet, but the first two, they were really good."

"I'm Cassidy, Sean's wife," Cassidy says, extending her hand in my direction.

"I know all about you too!" I shriek, unable to contain my excitement. I silently curse the beers under my breath and scold myself for oversharing.

"That's me," she says with a giggle. "I'm the muse."

"So aren't we," Hazel says, chuckling. "Book two has Ellie and me all over it. I'm still waiting for my autographed copy, Sean Anderson."

"Yes," I say. "You have both been through a ton. I've often wondered how much of the books is fact and how much is fiction. It's really neat that Sean was able to turn your stories into novels."

"Sean's book pretty much sums up my life," Hazel says, rubbing her hand on her abdomen and smiling up at Warren, who takes her hand in his and rubs her shoulder with his other.

"At least it had a happy ending," he says, his voice smooth and calming. He leans forward and kisses the top of her head.

"Very happy," Hazel says, pointing at her belly and laughing.

"So, your event-planning business… is that something you gave up when you moved up here?"

"Events by Hazel?" she asks, eyes wide. "No, I still have the Florida location. My assistant Sidone was promoted to manager. We have a York office as well, and that's where I work full-time."

"Wow!" I exclaim. "That's amazing. How do you find time to run two businesses and be a mom to Ellie?" I ask, swigging my beer faster than I intend. "And grow a human?"

"I have a lot of help," she says, locking eyes with Warren. "I've learned over the years that I don't have to do it all myself, and that's okay."

I nod and think about this for a beat, since Hazel and I

have similar stories. Well, not exactly similar... She was drugged at a frat party and ended up pregnant with Ellie, and fate just handed me Bex for no reason that I can figure out. However, we have both experienced lives as single parents, and just as Hazel had to learn to ask for help, I need to start doing the same.

"I can relate," I say. "I mean, my kid wasn't kidnapped from school and involved in a high-speed police chase... but... you know..."

"It's all good," Hazel says. "It all worked out for the best... and then some."

"Whatever happened to your nanny?" I ask, forgetting her name but remembering that she had much to do with Ellie's kidnapping.

"Gabby is doing great, thank God," she says, gathering her dark hair on top of her head in a messy bun. "She's getting the help she needs, and she's heading in the right direction, for sure... Actually, last time I spoke with her, she was passionate about helping people through addiction."

"That's incredible," Kayla, who has been listening silently, says with a serious expression. "Can we go on record that I successfully set Hazel and Warren up?"

"Because you were crazy jealous that she was my brother's ex!" I regret my words before they leave my lips. Both Lucas and Hazel shoot daggers with their eyes.

"Sorry," I say, gesturing to my red keg cup. "Blame the beer?"

"It's fine," Hazel says with a chuckle. "Your brother and I dated in another life. It's not weird at all... anymore."

"See," Sean says, gesturing in our direction. "I don't even need to brainstorm. There is so much history in this group I don't even need my own material."

Sean kisses Cassidy on the cheek, and she wraps her arm around his. "There is a lot of history in our family, for sure," she says. "I'm just glad that in the end things worked out for the best."

"You can say that again," Sean says, pulling her in for a giant squeeze.

"I'm just glad things worked out for the best."

"Very funny." Chuckling, he stands behind her and wraps his arms around her shoulders. *They are so in love it's nuts*, I think, not sure if I'm awestruck or jealous. Suddenly, my heartstrings are being pulled in multiple directions. Am I missing Noah? Am I longing for what we used to have, still mourning the loss of our relationship as I have done for the past six years? Or am I confused about Desmond? Still unsure about many logistics surrounding what our relationship could become? Sure, I love how he makes me feel... but a voice in the back of my mind screams that I am ridiculous to think that we could ever really be a thing, or whatever the kids are calling it these days.

"How long have you guys been married?" I ask, glancing at her diamond engagement ring and matching wedding band.

"About a year," Cassidy explains, smile beaming. "We were married at the Union Bluff Hotel, the same place—"

"The same place where your grandparents were married," I finish for them, recalling the story of Gwendoline and Gerry being married before his departure overseas. Of course, they didn't stay married, but regardless... this was obviously very special to Cassidy and Sean.

"That's right," Sean agrees.

"How is your grandmother?" I ask, thinking of Gwendoline Chase and hoping she is still alive and well.

"She's great," Cassidy sings, resting her head against Sean. "She's still living at West Valley Cove in the nursing home unit."

"Oh, I was just over there last week," I say. "I was visiting my son's great grandmother."

"They have been amazing with *my* grandmother," Cassidy exclaims. "Maggie Thatcher has really done wonders for her living situation."

I think for a moment, recalling the woman from the other day. "I just met her," I say. "She seems really great."

"Maggie is the best," Hazel adds. "I'm helping her plan her wedding."

"Really?" I ask.

"Yes, they are getting married in August. They have quite the story too."

"Book three," Sean says, winking.

"For real?" I ask, feeling like I need to pull my Kindle out right now and begin reading.

"For real," Cassidy and Hazel say in unison.

"Maggie's fiancé, West, works with me at my law firm downtown," Cassidy says. "He's really a great guy."

"It's such a small world," I say somewhat out loud and somewhat under my breath. I turn and face the cottage, looking for Des. My stomach fills with butterflies in anticipation of his arrival, and I blush when I think about our time together the other night. Kayla had swung by to pick up Bex, and she hadn't even completely pulled away from the cottage before Des was jogging up the stairs to the third floor, shirtless. I had been caught off guard, to say the least, because he barged into the kitchen and swept me off my feet before I could even muster up some sort of awkward greeting. We were in my bedroom and naked within minutes of his arrival, which was where we stayed for the entire night. Now I sip my beer and touch my fingers to the corners of my mouth to confirm that I'm smiling… and I am.

"Des?" Kayla asks.

"Yes, Kayla," I mutter under my breath. Desmond makes me smile.

"No, Tessa... is *that* Des?" she asks, nodding behind me toward the Anderson Cottage. The sun is starting to set, and I need to squint to focus on the man walking toward our circle of chairs. "He looks different than the picture," she notes. "Maybe it's because he's actually wearing clothes?"

I shake my head, and the beaming smile that was plastered across my face only seconds ago changes to a frown. All the beer I have consumed for the duration of the party begins to gurgle from within my gut, and my legs turn to jelly. "It doesn't look like Desmond because it's not Desmond," I say, my voice catching in my throat. Because strolling down the sandy hill toward me is a man I haven't seen in forever. A man I have tried to forget for the past six years. *Noah.* Noah is walking toward me, arms crossed over his chest, head down, clearly nervous, obviously on a mission.

"It's Noah," I say in a choked whisper. "What the hell is he doing here?"

IN THE PRESENT

DESMOND

July 2022

I've never really been the kind of guy with high hopes of settling down. I'm at my happiest when life is chill, and everything is simple. That was very true for me at the start of the summer. TJ hadn't been wrong. A few weeks ago, I was talking to a few different girls. Things were going smoothly, nobody was looking for a commitment, and I had the best of all the worlds. That was until I met them, and something changed. It's almost impossible to explain, but after I helped Bex and got to know her... I just felt like a better person. I like who I am when I'm with her... and it doesn't hurt that she is smoking hot.

To say things are happening fast would be a huge understatement. I feel like the connection we've developed after only a couple of short weeks has been stronger than anything I have ever experienced... which is crazy and not what I expected. But now, I'm afraid of screwing it up. The truth is,

I've never had a girlfriend. I want to go slow enough that I can navigate these feelings... feelings I've never had before with anyone, but I also can't control myself when I'm with her. She is different from the other girls... Maybe it's because she has her life in check, she knows what she wants, and she doesn't mess around. The girls I was talking to... they weren't like that. It's almost like they play games with my head... posting photos of themselves with different guys on social and then texting me to hang out. With TJ, I don't have to wonder where I stand... I know she's crazy about me because she tells me... Oh, she sure did tell me the other night... multiple times.

Which was why I fully intended on talking with her tonight at the Fourth of July party. I wanted her to hear it from me so that I could fully explain. My plan was to rent the Anderson Cottage until the end of August and then head out to Hawaii and settle down out there. I feel like I owe it to her and Bex... I don't know... Maybe it will change the way she feels about me? A part of me might consider staying local, if she wanted me to... but how insane would that be? Moving to Hawaii has been a dream of mine since I was old enough to run a Google search on the largest waves in the country. I knew how to surf before I learned how to read. I've dabbled in it competitively, but to really push myself and do what I want to do, Hawaii is clutch.

So, you could imagine my surprise when I showed up on the beach earlier this evening to find her standing there and staring at some guy, mouth gaping open in shock, arms crossed over her chest, basically trembling. A group of TJ's friends looked on nervously from their spot on the beach. "I just need to talk to you," he had said repeatedly. *Noah.* He was lankier and skinnier than I had expected. I could crush him with my pinkie finger with very little effort, and if she wanted me to, I would.

"What could you possibly need to talk to me about... It's been so long," she kept mumbling while shaking her head.

"Everything okay, bruh?" I had asked, flexing my arms and crossing them over my chest. I had realized that I was coming across as the stronger and more territorial type, but I didn't care. It had been the first time I'd seen her this upset, and I hated it. That had confirmed in my mind that I did really like this girl, a lot.

"It's okay," she said, grabbing for my arm and hugging it close to her body, her eyes welling up with tears. "I'm just... surprised, that's all."

"You must be Noah," I said, my words short and my tone sharper than normal.

"Yeah, that's right," the man had said, puffing out his chest and looking me up and down. "Can I help you?" If he could have growled at me, I was pretty sure he would have.

"Can *you* help *me*?" I chuckled, raising my eyebrows and smiling. "Dude, you better back off—"

"Or what?"

"Okay, okay," a guy from the party said, stepping in between Noah and me. "Let's just take a second and talk this through. You're a good guy, Noah... Nobody here is looking for a fight," he had said, looking in my direction. "You good?"

"I'm good," I had said, clinching my fist by my side.

"That's my brother," TJ had whispered in my ear. "He's cool."

"I just need to talk to you, Tess," Noah all but begged, his eyes pleading frantically. "There's just a lot I need to say."

Tess. I had come to know her only as TJ. My stomach had started to twist and turn in ways I didn't like, and my heart started racing faster and faster. "Then say it here," I had challenged.

"What are you, her boyfriend or something?" Noah had asked, the blood rushing to his face.

"And what if I am?" I had challenged, taking a step closer.

"Yes," TJ said in a choked whisper. "Desmond is my boyfriend. We're together... and whatever you have to say, you can say it to him too."

"How old is he? Like, twenty?"

"Twenty-three," she says, straight-faced.

"He's a baby, Tess."

"No, Noah... you're the baby. Des... he takes care of us. You... you bailed."

Now, as I sit next to TJ on the couch in the living room of the Anderson Cottage's third floor, she holds onto my hand for what feels like dear life. Noah sits across from us, beads of sweat forming across his forehead. His face is so pink from the blood that has rushed to his cheeks that he looks sunburned. TJ is perched next to me, looking fine as hell in that dress, and I must constantly remind myself to stay in the moment, not allowing my thoughts to wander back to the other night or *really* wanting Noah to leave so TJ and I can be alone together again. TJ's knee begins to bounce, and I gently place the palm of my hand on her leg, hoping to comfort her. *What the hell does this guy have to say that's so flipping important?* I think.

"I'm sorry, Tessa. I just needed to talk to you," he repeats over and over.

"Yeah. You've said that already," she says, rolling her eyes. "You could have called or texted... My number hasn't changed. Showing up here like this? It's just..." She shrugs.

"Creepy," I finish for her. "Showing up here is creepy."

"Fine," Noah agrees. "I'm sorry. I just, I haven't been myself lately, ever since you showed up on social."

TJ bites her lip and nods, clearly putting puzzle pieces together. "So, you saw my posts and couldn't be okay with us being happy?" *Us*, I thought. Was she referring to her and

Bex? Or her, Bex, and me? "I mean, I saw your posts, too, Noah. You haven't been very lonely."

"Nadine and I are taking some time," Noah explains.

"Some time?" she asks.

"Yeah, like a break, I guess. Listen, there are things I never told you... really serious and personal things, and until I do... I just can't... I just won't be okay... I can't move on."

"You already moved on," she says, throwing her hands in the air. "Noah, you bailed on me during the most difficult time in my life," she cries, her eyes welling up with tears. "One minute, you were going to propose, and the next, you vanished. It's like... it's like you were the one that died in that plane crash," she says between sobs. I wrap my arm around her shoulder and pull her close to me, keeping my eyes locked on Noah's and enjoying the way he squirms in his seat.

"I'm sorry," he says again. "I'm sorry for the way that went down. But please, let me explain."

"We're waiting," I say, my voice steady. "Go ahead and explain. We sure as hell aren't going anywhere."

IN THE PRESENT

TESSA

July 2022

Thank God for Desmond. I was crazy about him before, but just when I thought I couldn't take any more of this, of Noah sitting across from us and rambling on like a lunatic, Des placed his warm hand on my trembling knee. That confirmed what I already believed to be true, that he really was my guardian angel.

Now, as I lean my head on Desmond's shoulder, still listening to Noah go on and on about things I'm unable to process in the moment, I realize that I need to close my eyes. And although this comforts me in some ways, it doesn't fix the reality of the situation because the things that Noah is telling me are life-changing in ways that I just don't want to face.

Noah leans forward on the sofa and rubs his hands over his eyes. "I knew Samantha Allen," he says.

"What do you mean, you knew her?" I ask, my eyes remaining shut.

"I met her on a ski trip. My senior ski trip."

I gasp, thinking about Samantha's journal entries. Samantha never mentioned her mystery boy by name in her diary, but there was no denying she had fallen madly in love on that trip in a very short amount of time. "The one in Waterville Valley?" I ask, burying my face into Desmond's shoulder, suddenly very aware of where this conversation is heading.

"Yes," he says in a steady voice. "I slept with her… once."

My eyes shoot open, and I stare at Noah wide-eyed and hold onto Des so tight that I might be cutting off his circulation. "You slept with Samantha Allen on a ski trip that took place in December of 2009?"

"Yes."

"What are you saying?" I ask, although I know damn well what he is saying. I jump to my feet and begin pacing around the living room.

"I'm saying that there is a good chance I am Beckett's father."

I shake my head and throw my hands over it in defeat. "A good chance? A good chance you are the father? A good chance?"

"Yeah. A good chance."

"Because she was dating David when you slept with her!" I roar, obvious judgement written all over me.

"Yeah."

"Damn," Desmond says from his spot on the couch. "How could you let this go for so long?"

"Yeah," I say, agreeing with Des. "Why in the actual hell didn't you say anything?"

"Because!" he hollers, jumping to his feet. "Because I didn't know right away, Tess." He places his hands on either side of my face and locks his gaze steadily on mine. For a moment I am taken back to a time before my life was completely ripped away from me. I am twenty-three-year-old Tessa Walker, lost in the eyes of a man I loved more than life itself.

"You good, TJ?" Des asks from the sofa.

"Yeah. But I want some answers, now."

Noah nods and holds my face in his hands. "It happened once, on the ski trip, and I never saw her again. I didn't even know she ended up pregnant... I swear."

I inhale, exhale, and close my eyes. Just because Noah slept with Sam on the ski trip doesn't mean he is the father. But the things that Sam wrote in her journal were heavy things. She fell in love with another person on that trip... fast. Sort of like... sort of like what is now happening with Des and me. But another part of me is longing for this to be true... that Noah could be Bex's dad. But then where would that leave Des? I've felt more alive in the short couple of weeks that I've known him. And Bex? He's the best version of himself he's ever been. But it is all just too much to process in this moment. "Then how did you find out? What happened?"

"I was going to propose to you, Tessa."

My eyes shoot open, and my eyebrows rise. "I know," I confess. "And you stopped... *why?*" I ask, finally ready for answers after all these years. I step back and release his hands from mine.

"I saw her," he admits. "The night at the restaurant. I was taking the ring out of my pocket, and she walked behind you. She smiled at me and nodded and continued on."

"Okay?" I asked, wide-eyed. I remembered my encounter with Sam in the restaurant's bathroom, so his story lined up. "You were about to propose to the love of your life, and then you just froze because some chick you had a one-night fling with your senior year of high school strolled on by the table? And then you blamed it on *heartburn?*"

"Well, yeah," he said seriously. "I mean, that isn't all of it, but it was enough. After we slept together, I never saw her again. I thought about her a lot, I really... I really cared about her. I guess it just felt kind of like a sign that I saw her in that moment."

"A sign?"

"Yeah."

"What is the rest of it, if it wasn't all Samantha?"

"I wanted to go to medical school, and I thought you wouldn't want to move to Boston. There were a lot of layers to it, really... My mother—"

"Your mother hated me," I finish for him.

"You weren't her favorite," he admits.

"Dude," Desmond says from behind me.

I can't bring myself to look at him. If I do, I will break into a million pieces. I am sure of it.

"I was going to talk to you about all of that," he explains, his eyes beginning to water. "But when I got to your apartment that night, you had just received word of the plane crash. You had been notified that you were nominated for guardianship... Everything just fell apart."

"Tell me about it!" I shout. "*My* life fell apart. You left." I'm not sure what upsets me more, the fact that Noah and Samantha slept together, or that he might be my son's father, but does it really matter? Because the biggest tears I am crying are the same ones I have cried for six years. *He abandoned you*, a voice screams from deep within me. *It doesn't matter what happened prior to that. He abandoned you. He will do it again.*

"My life fell apart too," he insists. "I was going to stand by you and raise Bex. But then... I went to the funeral with you, and when I saw Samantha's face in her picture, I realized the connection, and I just... I just freaked out."

I shake my head in disbelief. "You didn't realize you were attending the funeral of someone you knew," I say, suddenly realizing how much of a shock that must have been for him. "Let alone someone that you... that you slept with."

"Right."

"How could you not know?"

"You never told me her name! You referred to her as Mrs. Allen, Beckett's mother."

"You didn't read the obituary?"

Noah shakes his head. "No, and even if I did, I didn't know her as Samantha Allen... I would have had to see her picture, and I didn't. Not until we were there, at the funeral."

"But you didn't have to leave," Desmond says, rising to his feet. "You should have told her."

"I know," Noah admits. "I just couldn't face it. I put all my energy into medical school, residency, and my career. Everything was fine... until I saw your pictures... and it just all became too much." Noah sobs and pulls away. A part of me feels sorry for him while another part wants to kill him.

"All this time?" I shout. "You might be his dad, and all this time you let me raise him... *alone?*" I clinch my fists by my sides as my heart rate increases. "You had answers," I say. "You had answers to why Sam would have left Bex to me. She left him to me because she thought we were getting married. She left him to me because she knew you could have been his dad. She carried that secret with her to her grave!" I scream, tears shooting out of my eyelids. "And you *left!*"

Des approaches from behind me and wraps his arms around my waist, preventing me from crumbling to the floor. "I'm sorry," Noah says.

"Sorry? You got your career... You got your dreams."

"And you got Bex," Desmond whispers in my ear. I turn

my face so that his breath is against my cheek, and I wrap my hands around his wrists, my heart beating so loudly that it is starting to hurt my head. "And she left him to *you*, not him," he says, gesturing in Noah's direction. "Because you can give him what he needs."

"I got Bex," I whisper back to Des.

"I got Bex," I say again, this time to Noah, firmly believing that I wouldn't change that, even if I had the choice. "And..." I say, looking from Desmond to Noah and back to Desmond. "And I have Des."

Noah looks down at the floor and shoves his hands into his pockets. I can tell I've hurt him, but I don't have enough left in me to care. "I get it," Noah says. "I'm sorry I let you guys down."

I think about this for a beat, sure there must be a better way of generalizing what he did to me... what he did to us. But I can't fight that battle, not now. Instead, I study Noah's face... his cheekbones... his eyes... his mouth... looking for any resemblance to my son, and I come up empty. "You don't even look like him," I say, clearly disgusted. "I've had about all I can take of this tonight."

"I know, Tess. I'm sorry."

"And what if he is yours? Are we all supposed to just ride off into the sunset as some big happy family?"

"I don't know," he says, shrugging. "I thought... I don't know... maybe?"

"Dude—" Desmond starts, his voice growing louder.

"Get out, Noah," I say, pointing at the door. "You're about six years too late."

* * *

About an hour has passed since I kicked Noah out of the Anderson Cottage. I didn't have enough energy to head back out to the party. Kayla, who had checked on me immediately following Noah's departure, assured me that she would keep an eye on Bex for the rest of the evening. "The fireworks might bother him," I had mentioned to Kayla. "He has noise-canceling headphones in his room."

"You're such a good mom," she had said, pulling me close in a tight squeeze. "That little boy is lucky to have you, even if it's for reasons you don't love."

"Thank you," I had said, removing my blue dress over my head, tossing it on the floor, and replacing it with my favorite T-shirt.

"Are you going to ask him for a paternity test?" she had asked.

I pulled down the covers of my bed and slid underneath, the sheets feeling cool against the warmth of my body, my eyes almost closing before my head hit the pillow. "No... yes... maybe? Who even knows?"

Kayla placed a water bottle on my nightstand and kissed the top of my head. "Whatever you decide, we've got your back."

"Thank you."

I had started to close my eyes, but Des entered the room just as Kayla was leaving. "Take good care of my girl," she had said.

"I got you," he replied. He closed the door behind him, removed his T-shirt and shorts, and climbed in bed next to me without saying a word. I shimmied my back against his torso as he wrapped his arms around my waist and snuggled his face against mine.

We haven't moved since. I feel the beating of his heart against my back, and although my mind is spiraling downward, my heart has never been happier... and at the same time... never been so broken.

"Des," I whisper in the darkness. "You awake?"

He doesn't answer, so instead, I listen to the steady rhythm of his breath, allowing it to comfort me. I'm still unable to process the bomb that Noah just dropped, and the worst part is, in hindsight, how did I not see it coming? Was it random that Sam Allen had been at the restaurant the night that he was supposed to propose? How do I know that she hadn't tracked him down, determined to ruin his life for the one-night stand? Or maybe she was just curious about Noah. Could she have been trying to talk to him about a paternity test? She had been so captivated by our photo by the Nubble. I had assumed it was the lighthouse she had been remembering so fondly... but it wasn't. It was my soon-to-be fiancé she was drooling over.

My stomach turns. For a moment, I regret all the beer I've consumed this evening. I lean into Desmond and wrap his arms around me tighter, so thankful for him, once again. "Where have you been all my life?" I whisper. "You're just too good to be true." I shove the thoughts of Noah and a possible paternity test out of my mind as best as I can. I'm not sure if I want any more information about the Allen family, but once again I am torn... because don't I owe it to Bex to figure it out? I decide that I will pay a visit to Wendy Jones at the retirement center again, hopeful that she might have more information for me, if I choose to look for it. But for now, I drift away to sleep, counting my blessings for the good that has come out of the chaos and deciding that no matter how uphill this battle has been, I'll never regret fighting it, since it has led me here... to this queen-sized bed on the third floor of the Anderson Cottage, wrapped in the arms of the best man I have had the chance to know... and it is exactly where I need to be.

IN THE FUTURE -

WRITER SALT PODCAST WITH SEAN ANDERSON

Sean: I remember that night like it was yesterday.

Tessa: *(laughing)* Well, I would hope so, you wrote an entire book about it.

Cassidy: I remember the look on your face. It was like you saw a ghost.

Tessa: That's pretty accurate... At the time, it felt like he was from a completely different life. Even though it was only six years, those six years were intense. I went from being a college graduate with my first job to the mother of a six-year-old boy.

Sean: So, a lot unfolded at the Fourth of July party. Not only did Noah show up, he confessed a lot of stuff he had been hiding from you. What were some of those things?

Tessa: *(sighs)* Well, he told me about the night of the ski trip. I knew right away what he was talking about because I read Sam's journal. Sam fell in love in a very short amount of time on that trip, and she lost that love as quickly as she found it. She described that time in her life as being "dark" and "empty" because she was burying a dream. And once I realized it was Noah she was referring to... I just got really... angry.

Sean: Yeah, you did.

Cassidy: With good reason. He should have told you about Samantha once he realized who she was. You had so many questions about why she left Bex to you, and all the while, he had an idea why. It's just so... awful.

Sean: Now, did it bother you that he slept with her? Or was it mostly because of the timing and the possibility of him being the dad?

Tessa: I mean, it's never great to hear that someone you care about has been with someone else. But that wasn't what bothered me... I didn't even know him at that point. What bothered me most was that he could have been the dad and he didn't tell me... He just... left. It also really upset me that Sam didn't disclose the truth while she was alive.

Sean: How do you feel about the fact that both Noah and Samantha fell for each other so quickly? Do you think that is a short time to know someone before you "love" them?

Tessa: I think every relationship is different. Do I think a week is fast? Yes. But the night of the party, Des and I had only known each other a short time at that point, and I fell for him hard.

Cassidy: It's like the summer of 2001 when I met Sean. We only had one summer together, but for the rest of my life, no matter who I dated or what life sent my way, I couldn't move past that summer with him.

Sean: *(laughs)* Well, yeah, babe. You left your fiancé at the altar.

Cassidy: Please don't remind me.

Tessa: So, yeah, I mean... I had a lot of emotions and questions the night of the party. There was a piece of me that was so happy to see him. That same part of me hoped that he was in fact Bex's father. The idea of the three of us being a family made my heart happy in ways I wasn't ready for.

Sean: And the other part?

Tessa: The other part of me wanted him to go away. I wished that he had never shown up and that I didn't have this information. But it's hard, too, you know? Because it isn't just about me. It's about Bex too. And although this is hard stuff, it's real stuff.

Sean: So you felt like you were being pulled in a bunch of different directions.

Tessa: In an overwhelming way.

Sean: At that point, after he disclosed *everything*... Was there any part of you that was ready to forgive him for leaving?

Tessa: That night? If I'm being honest... no. All I could see was the abandonment.

Sean: I can see that. But as someone who is very thankful for second chances, I had to ask.

Tessa: I can appreciate that. But you and Cassidy, you had a summer fling and broke up. This is a little different, right?

Sean: Totally. I get it. Let's rewind a bit... You found out that your ex might be your son's biological father. Was there a piece of you that wondered why Samantha didn't leave Bex with Noah?

Tessa: Oh, yes.

Sean: What did you do then?

Tessa: I paid a little visit to Wendy Jones over at Wells Valley Cove and demanded some answers.

IN THE PRESENT

TESSA

July 2022

"Good afternoon, and welcome to Wells Valley Cove and Retirement Center," Seth tells me without missing a beat. "Oh, hello again," he adds when he recognizes me. "You are down one tiny human," he says. I assume he is referring to the fact I am without my son.

"Yup," I say, brushing past him and walking towards the sign-in desk.

"What brings you here today?" he asks, following close behind.

"I'm visiting Wendy Jones," I say, walking faster. *The last thing I need in my life right now is another man,* I think to myself. *Especially Seth Jenson.* "Maggie knows I'm coming," I explain.

"How do you know Maggie?" Seth asks, raising his eyebrows. "Other than meeting her a couple of weeks ago?"

"Mutual friends," I say as I approach the desk. "Maggie

Thatcher knows I'm coming," I tell the woman behind it. "I'm here to visit Wendy Jones."

"Of course," she says. "Maggie will be right down." She hands me a visitor sticker, and I secure it to the corner of my blouse.

"Thank you," I say, turning my gaze out the large picture window and admiring the view.

"Welcome back, Tessa!" Maggie sings as she rounds the corner, full speed ahead. "So good to see you again."

"Same," I say, thankful for her friendly hug.

"Good afternoon, Miss Thatcher," Seth says with his toothy smile.

"Go away, Seth," Maggie says, shooing him away. "I'll take this from here."

"He sure is… eager…" I say.

"Oh, that's one word to describe him," Maggie says with a chuckle. "Come on, Wendy is outside, waiting for you. Cassidy and Hazel filled me in a bit… Are you okay?" I follow her down the corridor of WVC and down the stairs that lead to outside.

"Sort of," I say. "Just really confused, I guess."

"I can imagine," she says as we jog down the staircase.

"Can I ask you something?"

"Sure!"

"Wendy's granddaughter, Samantha. Did she visit Wendy often?"

Maggie pauses for a beat before opening the outside door. "She visited from time to time."

"And she never brought Bex?" I asked, finding this a bit odd.

"Not that I can remember," she says. "But that doesn't mean she didn't."

"I'm just trying to put the pieces together," I say with a sigh.

"This must be hard," Maggie says, lowering her voice as we head outside. "I know you have a million questions... I can't even imagine what you are going through. I know Wendy comes across like she's feeling great and has a good handle on things, but the truth is, she's been through a whole lot... you know, losing her daughter so young and then her granddaughter. She has her good days and her bad days."

"I got you." I smile to myself as I think about Desmond. "I'll go easy on her," I say with a wink.

"Thanks," she says, breathing a sigh of relief. "It's tough. I care about these residents like they are my own family."

"I know you do; it shows."

"Wendy!" Maggie sings. "You have a visitor!"

Wendy is seated under an umbrella at a table in the outdoor café, sipping tea. She wears white capri pants and a hot-pink top and matching lipstick. "Wendy," I say, reaching down for a quick embrace. "I love your hair." I sit across from her at the table.

"Thank you, Tessa," she says, fluffing the backs of her short silver curls with her palm. "I just got it done."

"You look beautiful as always, Mrs. Jones," Maggie says, blowing her a kiss. "You two have a good visit." She winks at me.

"Thank you," I say, watching her head back inside.

"It's lovely seeing you again," Wendy says. "I assume you read Samantha's journal and have some questions?"

"Yeah. That's exactly right. That, and my ex-boyfriend showed up at my beach cottage. And he's pretty sure he's Bex's real father."

"Your ex-boyfriend?" she asks, sipping her tea and closing her eyes for a beat.

"Yeah. He's apparently the guy from the ski trip. Do you... do you know anything about that?" I ask.

"Actually, I do. It's just... I think you are going to be disappointed."

"You do?"

"Yes, dear. Because if you are looking to find out who the real father is, I'm afraid you aren't alone. The truth is, Samantha never even knew the answer to your question."

"She didn't?" My eyes widen.

"Nope. I warned that girl before she went on that ski trip... no making babies... and she sure as heck didn't listen to me." Wendy sighs.

"What *do* you know?" I ask, hopeful this visit isn't a complete wash and trying to shake the image of Noah and Sam making a baby out of my mind. "About Samantha's relationship to Noah?"

"I can tell you that she fell for him hard... and fast. My Samantha didn't sleep around. She wasn't like that. And David, he was wonderful, always the provider... but lacking in some areas... He didn't always show up... emotionally." She chose her words carefully, like she was worried he could hear her.

"Okay," I said. "So, Samantha falls for Noah... She cheats on her boyfriend... That means she slept with both Noah and David in the same week... so why didn't she ever reach out to Noah?" I ask, rubbing the nape of my neck.

"You read the journal, right?"

"Yes, I did," I say, my bottom lip beginning to quiver.

"It wasn't about *just* her anymore. She wanted to protect her baby. David, he never knew about Noah. Samantha never told him about that evening on the ski trip... She never told him about the *cheating*."

"Okay," I start, but I stop and start again. "But then why did she just show up out of nowhere six years later?" I ask, my voice growing louder than I intend. "She came to my school and saw a photograph of Noah and me together, and then she decided that I was the best fit to raise her son?"

"That's right," Wendy says. "It's all just so... so... complicated. From what I know, Samantha loved her husband, but a piece of her always belonged to Noah."

"How is that possible?" I ask, a slight judgement in my tone. "When they only knew each other for a week?" But even before I finish saying this out loud, I realize what a hypocrite I sound like, because if Des were to suddenly disappear from my life at the drop of a hat, I would be devastated.

"I've learned a lot in my old age," Wendy says, sighing. "The truth is love doesn't discriminate. It happens to people in so many ways, at different times... It doesn't play fair." She cites Samantha's journal entry.

I nod, but I cringe at the thought of Samantha being with Noah, something I still haven't been able to process, and I recall her journal entries. *Can ninety percent of my heart belong to one person and the other ten percent belong to the other?* A wave of nausea sweeps over me, and I cross my arms over my chest and am suddenly speechless. *Can ninety percent of my heart belong to one person and the other ten percent belong to the other?* I repeat to myself, and suddenly my mind is blown because between Noah and Des, I have found myself in the same situation as Samantha—minus the pregnancy, thank God. But if I had to choose one of them right now, whom would I choose? And on top of that, I haven't learned anything new... just that Samantha loved Noah, which doesn't help. It might even make it worse.

"Are you okay, Dear?"

"No," I answer, resting my chin on my hand and peering up at her with watering eyes. "All this time... all this time I thought she left Bex to me because of the work I did with him... because I was helping him," I say, wiping a tear from the corner of my eye.

Wendy places a gentle hand on my forearm. "Don't discredit yourself," she says in a soft tone. "That was part of the reason. You see, she and David were traveling to Europe for their anniversary, but Samantha had plans to tell him *everything* while they were there."

"Everything?"

"Yes, everything. She was going to tell him about Noah. She was getting ready to ask him for a paternity test. When they met to discuss their legal affairs prior to their departure, Samantha told David and their attorney that she was interested in making some minor adjustments in the will. At the time, the nominated guardian was David's sister, whom he hadn't spoken to in years. If something happened to both at the same time, Bex would have gone to her."

"But why leave him to me, then?" I ask, openly frustrated. "Why not leave him to Noah?"

Wendy tilts her head and thinks for a beat. "If you ask me, Samantha used *your* name instead of Noah's because she was able to buy herself some time. She was able to put Bex in the position to be with both you and Noah without showing all of her cards to David."

I sit back and cross my arms over my chest. "It would make sense," I say. "So even if the plane hadn't crashed..." I suddenly feel horribly guilty for bringing this up. "I'm sorry." My voice catches in my throat. "I'm really a nice person. This is just all so much."

"It's okay," she says, pressing her hot-pink lips together. "Go on."

"Even if none of that happened... to Samantha and David... Samantha was about to blow everything up between Noah and me."

"Yes, that is correct. I believe that if Samantha and David

made it to Europe and back, her next stop would have been to leave David and to ask Noah for a paternity test."

"Wow." I shake my head, my mind completely blown. "Was she… was she hopeful? That Noah was the father?" I ask, thinking about the irony of the situation, since I, too, am wondering how I feel about him being the father or not.

"It's only speculation," Wendy says, choosing her words carefully. "But based on conversations I had with Samantha before she went on her trip, I would say that yes… there was a piece of her that really wanted Noah to be the father… even if just a tiny piece."

"I see." I take a deep breath and struggle to process this information, suddenly overwhelmed with curiosity. If Samantha and David hadn't died in the plane crash, was Samantha's next move going to be on Noah? Was that why she was randomly at the restaurant the night he almost proposed? My guess would be yes, that Samantha was indeed interested in Noah. Now it occurs to me that I'm not overly confident he would have chosen me over Samantha if their connection was as strong as she claimed it to be.

"Is there anything I can do?" Wendy asks, taking my hand in hers.

I shake my head and wipe my tears with the back of my free hand. "No," I say, suddenly eager to get back to the Anderson Cottage. "I just… I need to figure out what I'm going to do." My tears are now flowing freely.

Wendy reaches into her large brightly colored pocketbook and retrieves a tissue. She hands it to me and gently rubs my arm. "Can I give you some advice?" she asks, lowering her voice to a soft whisper.

"Sure, why not?" I ask, chuckling a bit and shrugging my shoulders.

"This is something that I should have told Samantha." She keeps her gaze locked on mine. "Follow your heart, dear.

Forget, for a moment, about everyone else... and follow your heart."

"I... I appreciate that, Wendy, I really do. But I *have* to think about my son."

"Samantha said the same thing. She spent six years of her life with David because she didn't want the conflict... She wanted what was best for Bex. But the truth was, she shared a special connection with another man, and she never got the chance to explore it. What a waste of love, of life!" she exclaims passionately, slapping the table's edge with her open palm.

I cringe, realizing now that my tears aren't over Samantha and David but for Desmond and Noah, and I can no longer hold them back. Although I want this all to go away, it is completely out of my control. I need to figure out what I want, and I need to make the decision based on myself. The concept of doing this disturbs me in ways I can't even start to process, because Bex, my son, continues to remain at the forefront of my mind, and I cry harder. "I don't know what to do." I throw my hands over my head in defeat. "I owe it to Bex to find out the truth, but I can't... I can't bring myself to find out."

"Oh, Tessa," she says, reaching for another tissue and dabbing the tears out of my eyes. "I know it doesn't seem like it now, but it is all going to be okay."

I smile softly and allow the tenderness of this moment to comfort me. I picture Samantha breaking the news of her pregnancy to Wendy, how scared and confused she must have been. I imagine Wendy comforting her in this very same way. "She was lucky to have you," I say, my voice cracking a bit. "Samantha."

"Thank you, dear. I was lucky enough to have her."

"I'm thankful for you, Wendy. I really am. I'm sorry to be such a bother."

"You are anything but that, Tessa. You are a blessing to my great grandson, to my family. And even though this shenanigan of hers didn't work out in the way I believe she intended... I truly believe that she is smiling down on you both... and I know without a doubt, she would be happy with the decision she made."

"That's really sweet of you," I say, blowing my nose into the tissue. "I'll be okay. Bex will be too. I just need... I need to figure out what the hell I'm supposed to do?" I ask more than say. "If he is the father..." My voice catches in my throat. "If Noah is the father, then I should give him a second chance, right?" I close my eyes and inhale deeply.

"I can't tell you what to do, and I don't have all the answers."

"I know—"

"Take some time. Nothing must be decided this instant. Timing..."

I think about Samantha's journal entry.

"Timing can be everything," I say. *And in this case, it's my enemy.*

IN THE PRESENT

DESMOND

July 2022

*I*t has been over a week since the Fourth of July party, over a week since Noah blew everything up. To say that TJ had a rough go of it would be an understatement, for sure. Of course, I don't know everything she and Wendy talked about that day, but what I do know is that TJ has changed a bit since Noah's visit, or it at least seems that way. She had returned to the Anderson Cottage after talking with Wendy and asked if I would watch Bex for a while. I took him for ice cream on Short Sands Beach, and we spent an hour at the arcade gathering up more tickets than we could even count. When I returned to the cottage, I found her curled up in a ball on the floor of her bedroom, sobbing uncontrollably. "TJ? What's wrong?" I had asked, closing her bedroom door behind me to give her some privacy.

"I asked him for it," she sobbed.

"Asked who? For what?" I asked, kneeling beside her and rubbing her trembling back.

"Noah! I asked him to do the paternity test."

No way, I had thought as I ran my free hand through my hair, suddenly wishing that she could take it back, take it all back. Suddenly overcome with fear and worry over what this could mean for me, what it could mean for... for us. "It's... it's okay," I whispered. I had leaned forward and kissed her on the cheek, wiping her tears away with my lips. But was it okay?

Now, we stroll hand in hand on Long Sands Beach, the sun setting in the distance as we admire the Nubble Lighthouse. I can't shake the worry or the fear, two emotions I have gone without having to deal with. Because over the past few weeks I've learned that it's easy to skip out on dealing with your emotions when you have absolutely nothing to be emotional about. Part of me longs for the days when I wasn't attached to anyone or anything... but then I look at her, at TJ, and I know instantly these thoughts are lies. Because she is stunning... inside and out, and all I want is to be around her... her and Bex, and the thought of losing them now is completely petrifying.

"Dinner was incredible," she says, swinging our hands as she walks beside me. The tide has gone out, and the sand is hard and cold against our toes.

I stop in our tracks and take her hands in mine. "You're incredible," I say, tilting my head to the side and raising my eyebrows, my mouth forming a smile I know she can't resist.

"You're such a flirt," she says, laughing. "Those eyes are going to get you into trouble someday." She pulls her hands from mine and gathers her brown hair over one shoulder.

"Dude," I say, laughing softly. "They already have." I take her by the waist and pull her close to me, her copper eyes locked on mine.

She stands on her tiptoes and plants a soft kiss on my cheek. "What do you mean?"

"Oh, I think you know what I mean."

"I'm not trouble," she says with a pout.

"No, you're not," I say with a sigh, wrapping my arms around her shoulders and squeezing her tight against me. I press my face into the top of her head and inhale deeply, taking in the smell of her favorite coconut oil shampoo, a scent I will never forget as long as I live. "But your situation is kind of messy," I say with a chuckle.

"Facts," she whispers into my chest. "I'm a mess."

"You're not a mess," I whisper in her ear. "You are perfect."

She pulls back and stares up at me then rests her head back on my chest. "This sunset is perfect," she says. "I wish every night could be like this. I wish we could stay here forever... and not..."

I can tell she is worried about tomorrow, since the paternity test results should be in. I hold her tighter, our eyes locked on the Nubble in the distance. "It's going to be fine," I say. "No matter what, I've got your back."

"Thank you," she says. "Where did I find you?"

"Sandy Toes Surf Shop, baby," I say, trying my hardest to get her to laugh, and it works. But a feeling of dread is forming in my gut, and I wonder whether she wants Noah to be the father or not. I don't dare ask this question because it is such a sensitive subject, and I'm trying to cheer her up.

"That's right," she says, squeezing me close. "I hated you that day."

"What?" I say, throwing my head back and laughing more loudly than I mean to. "That's messed up."

"You were kind of pushy," she says with a teasing smile. She plays with the bottom of her dress and spins around, pulling me close to her once more.

I tuck her hair behind her ear and kiss her gently on the forehead. "But you like me now, don't you?"

"Yes," she says. "It's kind of hard not to like you."

"It's kind of hard not to like you too," I agree.

"Sam's journal," she says, eyes fixed on the horizon. "There is this part I can't stop thinking about."

"Which part?"

"Samantha is referring to Noah and David." She cringes for a second. "She says that you can't love two people. She asks herself, 'How can I love one person with ninety percent of my heart and still have ten percent belong to someone else?'"

"That's... that's intense. And probably really hard for you to hear."

"Yeah."

"Who do you think was the ninety percent?" I ask, hoping my question isn't too personal.

"Well, at first I thought David, but after talking with Wendy... I just don't know."

"Fair."

"Do you... do you think that it's completely insane that they fell for each other so hard? In such a short amount of time?"

I think about this for a moment, suddenly very aware that she isn't just talking about Noah and Samantha but could very well be referring to *us*. "Are you asking about them... or about you and me?"

I hear her breath catch in her throat, and she takes a step backward. "I... I was talking about them," she says, biting on her lower lip. "But yeah. I guess I could be talking about us too."

"Well, I'm not an expert," I say. "But if they had anything comparable to what I have with you... then I don't think they were insane."

She thinks about this and nods. "Thank you."

"For what?"

"Oh, gosh." She laughs. "For what? For everything!" she says, shaking her head and shuddering with laughter. "Des, you have changed my life. You made me question *everything.* You don't get it, do you? You've changed me... You've changed us."

"You've changed me too," I say, pulling her close. *But how much of your heart am I entitled to?* I want to ask. *Are you fifty-fifty? Eighty-twenty? Ninety-ten?* I consider asking these questions, but she is smiling, and when she smiles... I... I forget everything. "Here," I say, squatting down and digging the tip of my pointer finger into the earth.

"What are you doing?"

"Watch," I say as I draw a heart in the sand.

"You made a heart," she says in her teacher voice. "Great work."

I stand up and wipe my hand on the side of my pants. "Not just any heart," I say. "It's my heart."

"It is?"

"It is. And... and I want you to know that no matter what happens tomorrow, or... or whatever you decide to do with your life... you will always have my heart," I say, placing her hand over my chest.

"Des, that's—"

"All of it," I say, keeping my voice steady and trying with all my being to fight back my tears. "One hundred percent, Tessa."

"You never call me Tessa."

"One hundred percent," I say again.

"Des... I... I don't know what—"

Her words are cut short because coming up behind her are some girls that I know a little too well. They have drinks in hand, and it only takes a second to figure out that they are completely wasted.

"Yo! Des! Surf's up!" Jasmine shouts as she approaches, arm in arm with Kamala. I can tell right away that TJ recognizes them, because she spotted them leaving the cottage before we met.

"What's up," I say, trying my best to play it cool despite being annoyed.

"What's up," Kamala repeats, stumbling over Jasmine and bumping into TJ.

"This is TJ."

They burst out in laughter and struggle to hold each other up. "TJ?" Jasmine twirls a strand of red hair around her fingertip. "Is that a nickname or something?"

"Nice to meet you," Kamala says, extending her hand out to TJ for a wobbly handshake. "I'm Kami. He was sleeping with both of us… before… before you."

TJ rolls her eyes, obviously unimpressed. "Nice," she says with a sigh, glaring at me out of the corner of her eye. "It's getting dark," she says. "We should go."

"Did he tell you about Hawaii?" Jasmine asks, hands on hips.

Shit, I think, knowing that this is not going to end well for anyone. "We will see you ladies later," I say, taking TJ's hand in mine and turning away from them, suddenly wondering what I even saw in them to begin with.

"What about Hawaii?" TJ asks, eyebrows raised.

"Desmond," Kamala says, eyes wide, "has dreams to move to Hawaii. He leaves at the end of August," she says, obviously satisfied with herself. "Aloha, Des!" she says, cracking herself up.

But TJ isn't laughing. In fact, her bottom lip is starting to quiver, and I think she might burst into tears. "Is that true? Are you moving?"

"I... uh..."

"So yes? Were you going to tell me? Tell us?"

"Okay, then," Jasmine says, holding onto Kamala for support. "We're going to go now."

"No," TJ says, holding up her hand to stop them. "You stay. I'll go," she barks as she releases my hand and marches away.

"TJ, wait—" I call out, wanting so much to explain myself. I trail behind her, kicking up sand as I trudge up the hill towards the cottage.

"Don't follow me," she calls back.

"Please," I beg. "Please let me explain."

"There is nothing to explain! You're going to Hawaii! Congratulations." She storms across the street and around the back of the Anderson Cottage. She scurries up the back porch steps to the third floor and pauses before entering. "I just... I just need some space, Des. I'm sorry." With that, she slams the door, leaving me at the bottom of the steps with my hands in my pockets and lots of regret.

IN THE PRESENT

TESSA

July 2022

The Nubble Lighthouse. A place that holds so much history, more than I can even begin to imagine. I learned about some of it in elementary school and at the York History Museum, but most of it I have come to know through Sean Anderson's novels. Stories of love lost and found, right here in the very spot I am sitting in now... on this bench... admiring the setting sun and the orange sky that serves as the perfect backdrop to the quaint little lighthouse that I have grown to love.

Gwendoline and Joey's story drew me in first, and if Sean's descriptions were accurate, it was in this very spot that Gerry found out about Joey and Gwendoline's affair and broke the news about his own. It was also right here on the rocks below me where Emeline met Jason while she was painting a picture of the lighthouse. And, in this very spot,

Lucas and Hazel broke up, and my brother's heart shattered into a million pieces.

I close my eyes and inhale the salty sea air. The ocean water crashing against the rocky hill soothes my tired soul. I rub my hand over my jeans to stop my leg from trembling and grasp the envelope in the other. For a moment, I wonder how my Nubble Lighthouse story will unfold. Will I get my happily ever after like Gwendoline, Gerry, and Joey? Will I be swept off my feet like Jason did to Emiline? Or will I be left here, alone, when all is said and done, like Lucas? One thing is for sure. My story is coming full circle tonight. Because inside the envelope I am holding are the results of the paternity test. And Noah will be here any moment to open it with me.

I place the envelope down on the bench beside me and scroll through my texts to pass the time. I have unread messages from both Kayla and Desmond. Kayla is just checking on me, and Des continues insisting that we *need* to talk. Hawaii was only a misunderstanding. It has been just about twenty-four hours since I fled from him on Long Sands Beach, and I've been avoiding him since. Part of me feels ridiculous for convincing myself that I could have anything *real* with Des. We are at two completely different phases in our lives, after all. If he has big dreams to pack up and go to Hawaii, then he *should* be able to go. He's not tied down to anyone, not like I am with Bex. I just don't understand why he wouldn't tell me he was going. And why does it hurt so much to think of him leaving? I haven't known him very long, and clearly, I'm not the only one he's interested in. A wave of nausea washes over me as I recall Jasmine and Kami and the way they looked at me... with pity in their eyes. Of course, they were probably getting a kick out of the fact that I believed Desmond would settle down with anyone, especially me. I understand that the anger and deception I am feeling towards Des is one hundred percent accompanied by an agonizing amount of jealousy. Not only are Kami and Jasmine much younger than me, but they are also both gorgeous. And aside from both being size-zero model-body types, they must be more fun than me, right? I mean, I'm basically living the life of a single mother in her forties, not someone his age. What did he see in me anyway?

I reach into my bag and remove my gray zip-up hoodie, surprised by how cool the air has become. I put the hoodie on and zip it up, rubbing my hands on my arms to warm myself. I glance around the parking lot and still don't see any sign of Noah. There are people around, some taking photos of the lighthouse and the sunset, while others sit on benches and rocks, like I'm doing. I had chosen this location for a few reasons, one being I didn't really want to be alone with Noah—not yet, anyway. The other was that I need to be away from the Anderson Cottage. I need space from Des and Bex.

"Hey," Noah says, approaching my bench quickly and without warning.

I freeze and stare up at him with wide eyes, a bit shocked that he has appeared out of nowhere. "I... I didn't see you coming," I say, suddenly embarrassed by the tremble in my voice.

"Sorry," he says, his tone harsh and unfamiliar. "Can I sit down?"

I pick up the envelope and gesture for him to have a seat. He does. Our space is limited, causing our bodies to touch, and I feel my heart start to race faster, if that's even possible. He wears jeans and a blue-and-green-checkered button-down shirt. I study his expression, and I can see that he, too, is a nervous wreck. He's already sweating bullets and looks like he might vomit or run away screaming at any given moment. "So," I say, locking eyes with him. "This really sucks."

Noah nods his head and grips the bench's sides with his sweaty palms. "Sure does."

The tightness in my chest is overwhelming, and suddenly everything I planned to say has escaped from my mind. Thoughts race through my head at a million miles per hour, and if I weren't grasping an envelope that could possibly define my future, I might forget why we are even sitting here, on this bench, staring at one of my favorite landmarks in the world, under a setting sun. "Did you love her?"

"Samantha?"

"Yeah, Samantha."

Noah fidgets a bit and crosses his arms over his chest. "I feel like there is no right answer here," he says, choosing his words carefully.

"How about the truth?" I ask, louder than I mean to.

"I didn't know her long," he says, closing his eyes and shaking his head.

"That's not what I asked. I asked, did you love her?"

"Fine!" he says, jumping to his feet. "I loved her. Are you happy? I loved a girl that I knew for a week, and she's dead."

"Why are *you* angry with *me*?" I demand. "You're not the victim here, Noah. Sit down."

Noah sits back down and wipes the sweat off his face with the back of his palm. "Sorry."

"It's fine." *But is it fine?* I think. "Listen," I say, taking a deep breath. "I just want you to be honest with me. Honestly, I want nothing from you, Noah. Regardless of what the results of the paternity test are, I'm not expecting anything from you… not your time… not your money."

"Tessa, stop!" he says, throwing his arms over his head. "I'm not worried about you asking for child support."

"Then what are you worried about?" I ask, now standing in front of him, waving the envelope in his face. "Are you worried that you *are* the dad? Are you worried that you *aren't?*"

"I'm worried about losing you... again." His expression softens. "Sure, I'm worried that I'm the dad... because that would mean that I bailed on my... on my son," he says, choking back an unexpected sob. "And I'm worried that I'm not the dad... because... because I want you to want to be with me, Tessa." He removes the envelope from my fingertips and places it gently on the bench. Then he takes my hands in his and draws me close. "I've missed you so much," he says, his voice quivering. "I don't want to lose you again... and I'm afraid that whatever is in that envelope is going to make or break us."

"Noah," I say, shaking my head. "I didn't leave... You did. And not only did you leave me, but you also left Bex. The past six years have been extremely difficult for both of us, so you're right... I don't have a lot of answers right now... and yeah, whatever is in the envelope is going to be hard to process and understand... especially because I'm the one who had to uncover the lies that you and Samantha kept from the people you love. I'm the one who was... who was left behind." Tears well up in the corners of my eyes.

He separates his legs and pulls me close between them as he wraps his arms around my lower back. I'm startled for a beat but am quickly overcome with emotion as he buries his face in my chest and cries. "I'm so sorry," he says repeatedly. "If I could do things differently, I would."

"I know," I say, studying the sky as it changes from colorful and bright to black. "We can't change what happened. We need to look ahead... to... to the future."

Noah pulls back and stares up at me, his tear-streaked face now only visible by the Nubble's red glow. "Future?"

"Yes, the future," I say, my tone firm. "Because this is life, Noah... and it must go on. And Bex... he needs me... I'm his mom now. And after six years of only looking out for him... I'm just learning how to think about myself again," I say, wiping the tears off my face with my fingers, suddenly confusing myself over my own grief. Are these tears for Desmond or for Noah? Whom am I even crying over? I think of Des and the way Bex has taken to him. I think of his smile and the light that he carries with him everywhere he goes. The effect he has on people he meets without even realizing it. And then I think of Noah and the life that we planned out... the relationship I have mourned for an entire six years.

"I want to be your future," he says, wrapping his arms around me again.

I bend down and wrap my arms around his neck, allowing the familiarity of his embrace to comfort me. "You do?"

"Yes."

"And Bex?"

"What about him?"

"Do you want to be part of his future?" I pull back and search his sad eyes for answers. And when he doesn't say anything, I know his answer. "Noah?"

Noah bites his lip and looks up at the stars like he is searching for answers.

"Noah?" I ask again. "It's not a hard question."

"This is a complicated situation," he says, his tone becoming factual and firm.

"What's so complicated about it?" I ask, pulling back and placing my hands on my hips. "Bex and I... we are family. We are sort of a package deal... I'm his mother."

"I understand that. I really do. And if... if he's... mine..."

"What if he isn't?" But even as the words leave my trembling lips, I know the answer. Noah wants to be with me.... take care of Bex... if and only if he's the dad. "I can't believe you!" I cry, pacing back and forth across from the bench.

"You haven't changed a bit!" I crumble to the ground, suddenly feeling weak. I try to breathe, but it becomes increasingly difficult. I haven't had a panic attack in years, but I am surely having one now.

"Tessa," Noah says, coming up behind me and placing a hand on my shoulder. "That's not what I said!"

"Go away!" I order between breaths as the world spins around me and my vision becomes blurry. For a moment, I start to wonder what it might be like to close my eyes and never wake up again. But Bex and his precious little face appear at the forefront of my mind, accompanied by thoughts of Desmond. I think about that first day in the ocean, when he placed his hands on the sides of my face and asked if I trusted him. *Look at me,* he had said. *Do you trust me?* I imagine his blue eyes and the way they shoot through me like electricity... the way he makes me feel, and Earth stops spinning and my heart rate steadies.

"TJ?" I open my eyes, suddenly startled. Desmond's voice has escaped from my mind and now sounds very real.

"What are you doing here?" Noah barks.

I open my eyes. Standing over me is Des, inches away from Noah's face.

"Des," I cry, my voice sounding as weak as I feel.

"Back off, dude," Des warns, puffing out his chest and moving toward Noah until he takes a step back, hands in front of his face in surrender. Des keeps his eyes locked on Noah as he bends down next to me on the gravelly ground. He wipes my tears away with his fingers and moves my wet and matted hair out of my eyes.

"I'm fine," I say, allowing a larger-than-life sob to escape from within me.

"Oh yeah, you look fine," he says sarcastically. "This is exactly what I look like when I'm *fine.*"

"She's fine, man," Noah repeats. "We were just talking."

"Whatever, *man*."

"We... we were just talking about everything, that's all. It's a lot," I say, climbing to my feet and brushing off my jeans. "He's just nervous... about the test. I'm... I'm overreacting, really." Desmond reaches for my arm, but I take a step backward, looking from him to Noah and then closing my eyes.

"We were just about to open the results..." Noah says.

"Yeah," I agree, opening my eyes and taking a breath. "We are just sorting out some things... It's all fine."

"I got you," Des, says, softening his tone. "But before you do, there is something I have to say."

"Of course there is," Noah moans. He rubs his hand over his head and looks at the ground.

"What is it?" I ask as Des takes one of my hands in his and places the other on my shoulder. It's only now that I notice the desperation in his eyes and the eagerness in his voice.

"TJ..." he says, his eyes wide and glowing in the moonlight. "I know we haven't known each other a long time... and it sounds insane... but I... I'm falling in love with you." His voice turns to a choked whisper. "I love the way you light up when you are with Bex, and I love how hard you try with him... what you do for him... It's truly amazing.... and I love the way I feel when I'm with you... just being *near* you makes me feel things... things I've never felt before. I swear, TJ, I've never cared about anyone as much as I care for the two of you... and it's great, and it's awesome, but at the same time, it sucks because I've never cared so much before."

"Thank you," I say, wrapping my arms around his neck, forgetting for a second that Noah is standing there watching everything unfold. "I'm sorry about last night," I say, suddenly mad at myself for not hearing him out and giving up on us in the moment.

"No," he says, shaking his head. "Don't be sorry. Last night was messed up."

"Yeah, it was." I smile for the first time all night. "Totally messed up. Are you going to Hawaii?"

"That was the plan… until I met you."

"Oh."

"Yeah, oh."

I bury my face in his neck and close my eyes. "I don't want to keep you from your dreams."

"I know. But honestly, TJ, who even knows what the future holds? None of us are guaranteed tomorrow. It's not about having the most money or surfing the biggest waves, even… At the end of the day, it's about who we are with that matters most. And today… not having you… it's been one of the absolute worst days."

"I'm sorry."

"I'm sorry too."

"But Des, there is *so* much I need to consider. I… I just need a little bit of space and time to figure out what's best for me… what's best for Bex." I pull back from Desmond and cast a side glance at Noah, who has picked up the envelope from the bench.

"I hate to break this up," he barks, "but if it's okay with the two of you, I would like to find out if I'm Bex's father."

I study him now, suddenly becoming very aware that I just don't know this person anymore. "What if you are the dad, Noah? What will that even mean for you? What will that even mean for us?"

"I guess we will find out, won't we," he replies, tearing open the envelope as he speaks.

I grasp Desmond's hand and become frozen in time, pretty sure my heart has stopped beating altogether. I study him, his eyebrows as they rise, his hand as it trembles.

"What is it?" I ask. "What does it say?"

Noah takes a step back from me, eyes wide, mouth gaping open. "I'm… I'm the father. Bex… he's my son." I hear him speak and watch his mouth form words, but I am unable to process what he is saying because the world continues spinning and my knees grow weak. Noah emits a high-pitched anxious laugh and shoves the paper inches from my nose. I strain my eyes in an effort to read the results myself, but I can't. The letters and numbers on the page blend together, and I just can't see them. "I'm his father!" he shouts, more loudly this time. "What do you think of that, Tess?" He cheers, like he's watching the winning play of a basketball game.

"I think," I say, turning away from Des and grasping Noah's forearm. "I think I'm going to be sick." And with that, I lean forward and puke… directly on Noah's feet.

IN THE PRESENT

TESSA

August 2022

If you ask me, nothing is more beautiful than a wedding on the beach. And although I've seen them on TV and in the movies, I've never actually been to one in real life. So imagine my surprise when I received an invite through Cassidy and Sean to attend the wedding of Maggie Thatcher and her fiancé, West Young. West works at Cassidy's law office, and Hazel helped with planning the wedding. Maggie realized the connection and insisted that we *needed* to be there. Of course, I couldn't say no... and besides, I'll take any reason to show off my boyfriend for a night.

"It's so beautiful, isn't it?" I ask, admiring the view from the Union Bluff Hotel. We sit hand in hand amongst the other wedding guests, studying West as he stands at the altar, wearing one of the biggest smiles I've ever seen. He stands beside his grandfather, Art, under an arbor of beach roses and multicolored daisies. A harp player strums the chords to Christina Perry's "A Thousand Years," and my heart flutters in anticipation of Maggie's entrance. Maggie and West had been best friends for most of their lives, and it wasn't until they were older that they ended up together. My insides burst with joy for Maggie, because today she will get her happy ending.

"You're beautiful," he says.

I squeeze his hand and giggle. "I love weddings," I whisper.

"I know."

"There's Hazel," I say, pointing behind us. "Gosh, is she ready to pop or what?"

Hazel wears a black halter-top maternity dress and somehow still manages to march around the event with her iPad, directing orders in red high heels.

"Hopefully she can get through the ceremony before giving birth." He laughs in agreement.

"Hopefully," I say, nudging him playfully in the arm.

He rests his hand on my knee and stops it from shaking before I'm even aware that it is.

"Thanks," I say.

"I love the dress," he says, eyeing my strapless black cocktail dress and running his hand along my thigh.

"Thanks," I say. "It's not too short?"

"Nope. Not too short. Actually," he says, leaning in and cupping his hand over my ear, "I'm looking forward to taking it off of you."

"Stop," I say with a giggle. But I don't want him to stop. Because I, too, am eager to be alone with him again. "Did you book the flights?" I ask.

"I did," he says with a smirk. "Thanksgiving week, just like you said."

"I'm so excited. Bex is too."

"You sure you want to do this?"

"We aren't moving there… just yet," I say, nudging him playfully. "Just checking it out. And I've always wanted to go, so it's a win-win."

"I'm sweating bullets in this suit," he says, wiping beads of sweat from his forehead with his palm.

"I got you," I say, handing him a tissue and smiling.

"You do, don't you," he says with a smile. He dabs his forehead and tilts his head in my direction, raising his eyebrows and flaunting those eyes.

"Oh, I think it's starting!" I say, pointing behind us. "I think I see her," I squeal eager to catch a glimpse of Maggie, the bride.

I watch her exit the hotel lobby, following her wedding party. Hazel has mentioned that Maggie's sister, Jordan, is her maid of honor, and her niece, Hayden, is the flower girl. I can see the family resemblance amongst the three of them at first glance, but it is Maggie, the bride, who takes my breath away. Her white strapless A-line wedding gown flows effortlessly behind her, and her blond hair appears stunning in an elegant updo.

"She's beautiful!" I squeal. "I love weddings."

"And I love you."

"I love you too." I lean over and plant a kiss on the side of his freshly shaven chin.

"With how much?"

"Huh?"

"With how much… of your heart?" he asks with a wink.

"Oh, *one hundred percent*, for sure," I proclaim. "I love you, Desmond Spencer… with one hundred percent of my heart."

IN THE FUTURE

WRITER SALT PODCAST WITH SEAN ANDERSON

Sean: Tessa, we just want to say a huge thank you for coming on *Writer's Salt* and sharing your story. Also, thank you for allowing me to write an entire book about you. You are truly an inspiration... If there were more people like you, the world would be a better place.

Tessa: Aw, thank you, Sean. That's nice of you to say. You guys are the best. Do you have any other questions for me? I feel like we basically covered most of it...

Sean: Well, sure, I mean... I don't want to get too personal...

Cassidy: *(laughs)* I think we are past personal, babe.

Sean: True. Well, my readers did have questions. Mostly about Noah.

Tessa: Okay?

Sean: Well, we know that he is Bex's biological father, and we know that you decided not to pursue a romantic relationship with him.

Tessa: That's correct.

Sean: My readers have wondered... what ended up happening with him?

Tessa: *(chuckles)* Oh, don't worry about Noah. He's doing great... He has his hands full, but he's very *blessed,* I guess you could say.

Sean: Ha ha, yeah. I know what you are talking about, but you should probably explain.

Tessa: Right. He's engaged to the girl he was seeing from Boston, the one he met in medical school.

Cassidy: Barbie.

Tessa: *(laughs)* Right. They are engaged to be married, and... well, they have twins on the way... due any day now.

Cassidy: Good for them. Has he kept in touch with Bex?

Tessa: Oh yes. He has been extremely supportive in all the ways he can be. He FaceTimes with Bex a ton, but I don't think I'll get him to come out all this way anytime soon. But I was hoping that you and Cassidy could make it sometime?

Sean: Oh, man... we would love to come out to Hawaii. We've been following you guys on Insta, and it's just... wow... paradise is an understatement.

Tessa: You should! Come check out Desmond's shop! He's crushing it.

Sean: I'm sure he is. I heard you are too.

Tessa: Yes. I got the guidance counselor position at Bex's school. I'm absolutely loving it.

Cassidy: Congratulations, Tess!

Tessa: So yes, we would love to have you join us.

Sean: Never know, maybe we will come check it out. I could use some inspiration for book five.

Cassidy: *(clears throat)* Well... actually...

Sean: You want to tell her... now?

Tessa: Tell me what?

Sean: Well, speaking of congratulations... we have some news of our own.

Tessa: Stop it! Right now.

Cassidy: Yup.

Sean: Cassidy and I are expecting a baby girl in the fall. Not sure we will be jumping on a plane to Hawaii anytime soon, but we sure are excited.

Tessa: That's amazing! I'm so happy for you guys. This made my day. Thank you for sharing.

Sean: Thank you, Tessa. And thank you for coming on. Say hi to that little monkey of yours for us.

Tessa: I will... He's with Desmond out in the water now. I'm going to join them... We've been doing our share of surfing lately. Waves out here in Oahu are incredible.

Cassidy: Hawaii suits you, Tessa. It's nice to see you so happy.

Sean: I'm jealous! Catch some waves for me.

Tessa: I will. Thanks for having me and letting me share my story.

Cassidy: Thank you! I love your story... It has such a happy ending.

Tessa: It does, for sure. Aloha, guys.

Sean: Aloha, Tessa! Thanks, everyone, for listening. This is Sean Anderson, author of *Stories of the Nubble Light* and producer of *Writer Salt*. Hope you all have a great day. Sean and Cassidy signing off.

Cassidy: And baby Anderson!

Sean: Yes, and baby Anderson. You are the best, Cass.

Cassidy: No, Sean. You are, really. I love you so much, and I'm so proud of you... Hey, what are we doing for dinner? I was thinking we could hit the piano bar and then get ice cream downtown. I'm craving a banana split like my life depends on it. And then maybe get to bed on the early side? It's been a while since... you know...

Sean: Hey, Cass?

Cassidy: Yeah?

Sean: We are still online.

EPILOGUE

Dear Samantha,
It breaks my heart to know that as I write this, you will never read it... not in this lifetime, anyway. But still, I can't go another second without getting some things off my chest. Of course, it's a healthy way for me to process the changes and grief we have all endured over the years... but even more than that, there are things I need to say.

I realize now that falling in love with Noah was never your intention. You were obviously head over heels in love with David. And that reason alone is why you handled your situation in the way that you did. Yes, relationships take work, and each has its own unique challenges. I truly believe that you were happy and that working things out with David really felt right... especially for Bex.

In your journal, you mention that when you have feelings for a person, whether that be love, lust, or whatever... it is still real. I can't imagine what it must have been like for you to fall for Noah in such a short amount of time, especially being so committed to David. You are correct, love doesn't play nice... It can show up out of nowhere, when we least expect it. I know because it happened to me too.

You said, and I quote, So, if I can't very well dedicate ninety percent of my heart to one person and ten percent to another, where does that leave me? Oh, Samantha, I'll tell you where it leaves you. It leaves you six years into a marriage questioning whether or not you made the right choice. Committing to David when another man had a piece of your soul and believing you could move forward without ever looking back was probably your first mistake. Because not only did you fail to tell Noah how much you loved him, but Bex also missed out on an opportunity to know him. Noah is a lot of things, but when push comes to shove, he really is a great man. Aside from that, you kept a huge secret from your husband, and marriages and relationships built on a foundation of lies never work. Trust me, I do this for a living, I should know.

I know that you did the best you could in an impossible situation. Although I'm still confused about why you showed up that night at the restaurant and why you felt the need to sabotage my relationship when you did. Did you know he was going to propose? I must admit... I'm thankful for you, because if he had proposed to me that night, I would have said yes, and our marriage would have started like yours... based on untruths. In hindsight, you probably saved me a ton of pain. Aside from that, I never would have met Desmond, and I've never been happier. I firmly believe that he is the love of my life.

Thank you for leaving me Bex. I like to believe that out of all the choices you made during that time in your life, leaving your son to me was your best decision. He has changed my life, and I am forever grateful. I've enjoyed watching him grow, and I love him more than words can say. And you should know, when I teach him about love and when he bashfully talks to me about girls and romance, I tell him the truth. And this truth took me a while to learn, but I truly believe that knowing this will make his life complete. I tell him, "Bex, follow your heart, Dear. You need to listen to your heart and do what makes you happy. Put yourself first and continue to dream. Because the truth is, our hearts make us whole. We can't split them up like fractions or categorize them by percents. When you find your person, the love of your life, your soulmate, or whatever you want to call them, they will deserve one hundred percent of your heart and nothing less."

I'm sorry that I never got to know you. Sometimes I wonder if I could have been able to help you if our conversations could have moved past highlights and toothpicks or lighthouses and behavior plans. But I know that isn't true, because back then, I didn't know any better either. And besides... you are the one who helped me. Without Bex and without knowing your story, I never would have come to realize these things... but one thing is for certain... I will make sure he never forgets you.

Rest in peace, Samantha Allen. Maybe someday we will meet again. Until then, trust in the knowledge that not only am I taking care of Bex, but he is also taking care of me.

WITH LOVE,
Tessa
P.S. I got you.

ABOUT THE AUTHOR

Stacy Lee is the author of the Nubble Light Series. Stacy is a lifelong resident of New England. She lives in New Hampshire with her incredibly supportive husband, two beautiful children, and two well loved (spoiled) rescue pups. She enjoys spending time in the beautiful and historic town of York Beach, Maine with her family. The Nubble Lighthouse holds a special place in her heart.

Before she started writing women's fiction, Stacy received her bachelor's degree in elementary education with a teacher certification in grades K-8. She taught elementary school and writing courses to students for fourteen years while completing a graduate degree in elementary administration where she graduated with honors. After that, (in an effort to drive her husband completely crazy) decided to switch careers and go to Bible College, where she graduated with a Master's in Christian Ministry with a focus in Homiletics. Finally, when she got tired of taking college courses she decided to pursue her dream as an author. She is thankful for her husband and his ability to bring out the best in her...always.

BOOK FIVE OF THE NUBBLE LIGHT SERIES

MAID FOR SUMMER BY- STACY LEE

Does letting go mean giving up?

As a recent college graduate, Summer Jennings had ambitious career goals. After graduating at the top of her class, she was one step closer to becoming an elementary school music teacher. That was, until her best friend and college roommate Tessa Walker submitted a recording to a nationwide singing competition out of Hollywood, California on Summer's behalf. Against her parent's wishes, Summer fled to Hollywood to pursue her even bigger dream of becoming a famous singer and songwriter.

Now…in her early thirties, Summer has learned the hard way that life isn't always fair. After being chewed up and spit out by the entertainment industry, Summer retreats back to her hometown of York, Maine, where she decides to work for her family business- a quaint beachside motel on Long Sands Beach in the housekeeping department. Convinced that things are steamrolling in the wrong direction, Summer's life begins a downward spiral. That is until word gets out that famous local writer Sean Anderson has locked

BOOK FIVE OF THE NUBBLE LIGHT SERIES

in a movie deal for his award-winning novels, Stories of the Nubble Light, and Summer's longtime celebrity crush Lawson Remington has landed a leading role. What begins as an attempt for an innocent starstruck meet and greet turns into an adventure beyond her wildest dreams, as Summer realizes that sometimes letting go of one dream can mean embracing what she is truly meant for—and more.

ALSO BY STACY LEE

The Hundredth Time Around- Book one of the Nubble Light Series

Future Plans- Book two of the Nubble Light Series

Never in a Billion- Book three of the Nubble Light Series